FURY OF CONVICTION

COREENE CALLAHAN

1

WASHINGTON STATE – LAKE CHELAN

Standing in the kitchen of his hideaway, Hamersveld wiped down the countertops. From his position behind the small island, he scanned the one room cabin. Squared away. Everything in its place. Throw pillows lined up on the long couch facing the river rock fireplace. Hudson's Bay blanket folded over the back. Coffee table and comfortable armchairs positioned just right. King-size bed made, sitting snug against the side wall, complete with featherdown duvet, plump pillows, and clean sheets.

Neat.

Tidy.

Ready to serve a singular purpose—to impress his visitor.

Hamersveld frowned. Well, his *maybe* visitor. He didn't know yet. Kept going back and forth, struggling to decide. Logic suggested he could go either way— veer away from pack protocol and do the unthinkable. Or stay on the straight and narrow and ignore the problem.

Hard to do.

He'd been turning a blind-eye for weeks. Trying to make sense of his reaction to a female who wasn't his

—and never would be—but...nothing worked. He'd tried and failed to ignore her. Attraction, his inability to stay away, kept shoving reality in his face. Regret rose, burning through him like a long-tailed comet. Ignoring her—and the problem—was no longer an option. The injustice of the situation refused to leave him alone, poking at him, prodding his conscience, making him want to intervene, but...

Breaking her out, bringing her here—to his lakeside sanctuary in the wilds—was a bad idea. The absolute worst, given his tenuous position inside the Razorback pack. And yet, that's precisely what his dragon half wanted him to do—betray his new commander and help the female suffering inside Cellblock A.

Uncertainty washed through him.

He flexed his hands. The dishcloth dripped water between his fingers. Droplets splattered across the worn butcher block countertop. Full of OCD tendencies, his dragon half cleaned it up with a mental swipe. Water evaporated from the wooden top, leaving nothing but pristine surface behind. His mouth curved. Goddess love his magical side. His beast might not mind battle and blood, but on the home front, his better half despised mess. Liked things a certain way, insisting his environment remain tidy wherever he went.

Unable to deny the compulsion, Hamersveld folded the wet cloth and laid it neatly over the spine of the double sink. Stepping around the island, he surveyed the room again. A wall of windows looked out onto the rocky outcropping where he'd set his cabin down. A wide cedar deck cantilevered over the bluff, hanging over the cliff and the beach below, providing the perfect springboard whenever the urge to swim overtook him.

Which, given his proclivities, was often.

Footfalls muffled by thick area rugs, he skirted matching armchairs and approached the floor-to-ceiling windows. Moonlight glinted through the triple panes. Hemmed in by mountains, the narrow lake lay beyond, glinting beneath a starry sky, its calm surface coaxed into gentle ripples by a marauding north wind.

Mesmerized by the sight, Hamersveld stared at the dark blue water.

Tension released, cascading down his spine to flow, smooth as silk, through the soles of his feet. Taut muscles relaxed. Cracking his neck, he inhaled deep and exhaled long, his gaze on the view. He loved it here, lakeside, tucked between mountains and forest.

The single room cottage made for the perfect setup, reminding him of home. Of deep Nordic fjords, rough terrain, and seaside bonfires. The thought should've brought pangs of longing, but homesickness no longer came when he pictured his native Norway. Too much time had passed. Too much pain lay in that direction. Too many bad memories tainted the yearning most warriors felt when far from the land of their birth.

Here, though, in the wilds of America, he'd found his place. A lovely little getaway, a secret hidey-hole, far from glaring city lights and the demands of his new pack. Somewhere to escape after a long night and—

Hamersveld huffed.

Right. Sure. A nice idea, but an unlikely scenario.

Escaping to his cabin no longer happened on a regular basis.

He couldn't get away every day. Ivar needed him

inside the lair, corralling warriors, planning missions, overseeing the day-to-day operations of a busy Dragonkind pack. Why the hell had he agreed to become Ivar's first-in-command? Hamersveld sighed. No clue. He ought to have his head examined. Or say fuck it and fly out. Go somewhere else. Some place quieter, far from the constant demands.

A tempting proposition.

Total kneejerk reaction.

He already spent too much time alone. Had existed for centuries on the fringes of Dragonkind society, part of it, but not really. Until Ivar. The male was solid. Felt real to him in ways he didn't understand and couldn't quantify. His bond with the leader of the Razorbacks surprised him. The intensity of the connection—the honesty, kinship, and deep sense of brotherhood—spoke to him, urging him to stick with it.

The idea was startling.

The feeling was even worse.

Ivar trusted him. *Him.* A warrior most males feared and avoided. A water dragon with a bad track record, no ties to anyone—or anything—before Ivar reeled him in and gave him purpose. A cause to care about beyond Fen, his wren and only companion. A place to call home even though Hamersveld wasn't sure he deserved to belong anywhere.

Especially given what he'd done. What he continued to do every day.

He'd lied right out of the gate, giving Ivar a false sense of him. Normally, he wouldn't care. Rumors about him abounded—his lone dragon status, the undeniable brutality slithering through his veins, and the fact most of his kind believed he murdered females and his own children.

Untrue. A giant lie. One he'd refused to counter with the truth.

He didn't kill his own offspring. *Hristos*, he'd spent centuries trying to have one. Each time the Meridian realigned, he tried again. The cycle was never-ending —find a strong female, spend the night of the realignment with her, wait to see if she bore fruit, but...

Nothing ever happened.

Despite his best efforts, he remained childless. Alone in the world. Without the son he so desperately wanted.

Swallowing the lump in his throat, Hamersveld shook his head. So much heartache. Continual pain. The brutal reality of a dream unrealized. A yearning he set on the back burner most day, determined to ignore the ache. But with Ivar's plan in full swing, he couldn't turn a blind-eye anymore.

He should come clean.

Tell the truth.

Give his commander the information he needed.

And yet, he couldn't, and for some unfathomable reason, lying to Ivar bothered him. It wasn't about honesty. He wasn't above using deception when it served his purpose. Hell, he'd been doing it for years, pushing the myth, letting Dragonkind all over the world believe the worst about him. A good plan when dealing with untrustworthy males. Not so hot while trying to build a new life. After so many years on his own, he longed for community, for camaraderie—a launch pad into deeper connection with a warrior searching for the same.

Hamersveld clenched his teeth.

The idiocy couldn't go on.

He needed to be honest about the Nightfury.

Wanting to fit in, needing a safe place to land, he'd

misled Ivar, steering him toward rumor and away from fact. Mac—the Nightfury commander's water rat —didn't belong to his ancestral line. How did he know? The magical mark on the warrior's scales didn't match his own. Passed from sire to son, the tribal ink always *matched*—shape, size, location on the body, down to the millimeter. Which meant…

He hadn't sired the bastard.

Mac couldn't be his son.

Approaching the double doors, Hamersveld opened the pair with a mental flick. Well-oiled hinges hissed as the glass panels swung wide. Without pause, he strode over the threshold, out into moonlight. Boots thudding across cedar planks, he approached the deck edge and murmured a command. His clothes disappeared. Standing naked beneath the night sky, he tilted his head back and, skin steaming, basked in the cold March air.

Not long now.

Just three weeks until the Meridian realigned, and he'd be forced to decide.

About *her*. The redhead, she of the gorgeous energy. The female he shouldn't want, but couldn't keep from craving.

Flexing his hands, he murmured, "Fen."

Magic whispered against his skin. The tribal tattoo bracketing his spine rippled in response. Dark blue ink heated, smoothed into light grey, then started to glow. Light washed across the deck, painting tall pines and short shrubs as the wren reacted to his call.

Power pulsing in his veins. Hamersveld hummed. "Night's fallen. Time to move."

With a growl, the wren obeyed, separating from his skin. Feathers of black mist whirled around him as Fen took shape and form. Shadows turned to shark grey scales, dark wings, lethal claws, and glowing yellow eyes.

Hamersveld smiled as the miniature dragon hovered, waiting for the usual. Completing the greeting, he reached out to stroke Fen, caressing the collar of spikes ringing the wren's throat. During a fight, the blades would stand on end, but with no threat in sight, the lethal daggers lay flat against the side of his neck.

Drawing his thumb along the middle of Fen's snout, he scratched behind his horns. "Sleep well?"

Tilting his small head, Fen leaned into his touch, then chuffed in agreement.

"Good," he murmured, more concerned about Fen's rest than his own. Which was stupid. Without him, Fen would die. Bonded in the way of the Ancients, his life force kept the wren alive, plugging the miniature dragon into the Meridian—the electrostatic bands ringing the planet, the source of nourishment for all living things—allowing Fen to survive on Earth. "Time to fly."

"*Cascades?*" Fen asked, communicating the only way he could—through mind-speak.

Hamersveld nodded.

Putting it off any longer wasn't a good idea. As the Razorback's first-in-command, Ivar expected him to stay on top of things. To keep the warriors competing for the right to breed with one of Ivar's HE females in check. Held inside the city lair, the females were comfortable enough—well-treated, well-fed, given anything they wanted—though *held* was a nice way of putting it. *Imprisoned* was a better word.

Hamersveld rolled his shoulders, attacking the tension.

He didn't agree with Ivar's plan. Didn't like Cellblock A or the fact six high-energy females lived inside the comfortable complex. He'd never been one for harems—or the high walls and lack of freedom associated with the ancient custom. A subject he'd broached with Ivar more than once.

Not that he opposed the breeding program or his commander's objective.

The serum Ivar developed in his state-of-the-art laboratory was ingenious. Dragonkind needed females of their own. Being forced to rely on human females for sustenance couldn't continue long term. Too bad the Goddess of All Things was a vindictive bitch.

In a fit of temper, the goddess had lost her mind and done the unthinkable, making one race reliant on another to procreate, driving Dragonkind into an intolerable situation in order to survive. *Reliance*—the worse kind of insult for a breed stronger than any other species on the planet. So...no question. Ivar's instinct to end their dependence on humans amounted to a good one, but that didn't mean HE females needed to be imprisoned to achieve the goal.

At least, in his view.

Catch and release worked just as well.

Setting up a tracking system wouldn't take much effort. Locate an HE, inject her with the serum, without her being the wiser. Embed a tracking device beneath her skin. Follow individual subjects remotely, allow each to live her life unfettered, until the Meridian realigned. Little fuss, no muss. Problem solved. No need to curb a female's freedom...or take her life before the infant was born.

The ends, after all, didn't always justify the means.

He valued his freedom, which meant he must value another's. Otherwise, he was nothing but a hypocrite, and—

"Silfer's balls," he muttered, raking his hair away from his face.

He'd gone off the deep end. No way should he care this much. Giving a damn had never been his MO. And honestly? The manner in which Ivar set up the breeding problem wasn't his problem, and yet, he hated it. Despised watching the redhead suffer night after night.

He growled at the sky. "She's driven me mad, Fen. It's the only explanation."

"*Pretty girl. Pretty girl. Pretty girl,*" Fen said, parroting what Hamersveld thought every day.

"Yeah," he murmured, back to deliberating. Back to the uncertainty. Back to hoping the cabin was clean enough if he decided to break ranks and bring her to his sanctuary. Shaking his head, he waved the wren away. "Go."

Cold air blasted his bare chest as Fen wing-flapped, taking flight.

Hamersveld watched him wheel around the tops of tall pines, then called on his own magic. Water vapor swirling around him, he shifted from human to dragon form. Shark grey scales replaced his skin as his hands and feet turned to paws and claws. His night vision sparked. Sonar up and running, he sent an exploratory pulse. The surge gathered speed, spilling over rugged terrain, moulding over nearby towns, grabbing information to send back to him. Nothing and no one near him. Not surprising. The north end of the lake rarely saw action. Humans kept to the south end, enjoying the marina, fancy coffee shops and wineries instead of more mountainous terrain.

Wood planks groaning beneath his bulk, he tucked his wings and dove over the bluff. The bay winked below him and...

Splash-down.

Fresh water rushed over his smooth interlocking dragon skin. The jagged sawtooth fin along his spine cut through the water as he headed north. Swimming fast, he sliced through the narrows, snaking around jagged rocks in deep water, tracking Fen as the wren flew above him over the surface.

At the end of the lake, he ran out of real estate and, thrusting upward, exploded out of the water. Droplets blew off his scales, splashing into Chelan Lake as he rocketed into the night sky, banked right toward the Cascade mountain range, and the makeshift warrior camp nestled in the woodlands.

Fifteen minutes and some fast flying later, he slowed his roll to a smooth glide. Angling his wings, he scanned the ground, searching for the human military compound. Abandoned after WWII, trees and climbing vines grew around multiple structures, mounding over ancient round-topped airplane hangars, obscuring cracked concrete and most of the runway from the air. Deep depressions in the earth, though, remained. A testament to ingenuity and the enduring legacy of engineers from a long-forgotten era.

Thick forest gave way to open ground.

Hamersveld picked his spot and, folding his wings, dropped out of the sky.

Fen streaked overhead as his paws thumped down, making old, vine-infested army Jeeps jump and the steel doors leading into ancient barracks clang.

A warning to the males inside.

He didn't have time to mess around. Azrad needed to be shoved back into line. Though, that was asking a lot. The warrior was more than just difficult. He was lethal. Far too smart for his own good. Way too powerful to be ignored.

Something, in all honesty, he appreciated about the male.

Azrad was a warrior's warrior. A leader in the true sense of the word, but with the competition for HE females in full swing, the male wasn't leading so much as dominating.

Hamersveld understood the urge.

The need to win was in his blood, as much a part of him as swimming. So, yeah...he empathized, comprehending what drove the male. A shot at the title—the promise of spending quality time with an HE female, of being first to choose—was powerful incentive. Foreplay most Dragonkind males couldn't resist, but...

He needed to rein in the youngster, fast. Otherwise, Azrad would kill all his competition, leaving nothing but devastation and dragon ash in his wake.

His lips twitched at the thought.

A muffled clang drifted out the barrack doors.

Another crash. The unmistaken sound of cursing and fists meeting faces.

With a huff, Hamersveld shifted and conjured his clothes. "Fucking Azrad."

The male was in fine form tonight, beating the hell out of his fellow competitors before any of them took flight for the night. The contrary SOB needed an attitude adjustment. One he was primed to give after suffering through the uncertainty of what to do about *her*.

Three weeks until the Meridian realigned. A measly twenty-one days.

Not a lot of time. Such a monumental decision.

Sink or swim. Time to decide—betray Ivar in

order to set the redhead free. Or hold the line and remain faithful to the Razorback cause.

Shaking his head, Hamersveld put his boots in gear. He needed a distraction. Welcomed the coming brawl. Cracking heads would take his mind off the problem, and Azrad? Lucky male. He'd just put a bullseye on his chest, a target Hamersveld was only too happy to hammer.

2

Sitting cross-legged in the center of the queen size bed, Natalie Bainbridge stared at the floor-to-ceiling glass wall. Seamless. Spick and span. No spots to be found on the clear surface. An unlikely front for a prison cell. Then again, so was the inside. The beauty of her designated 'space'—the built-in desk and bookshelves, pale violet walls, soft area rugs and deep-seated armchair—screamed comfort. Invited a person to take a load off and stay awhile, but was all wrong.

A huge lie. Twisted in a lonely, tortured sort of way.

Lovely box, hellish existence.

The dichotomy—the push-pull between prison and pretty—strung her tight. Put her on an edge so sharp most days she didn't know what to expect...or which way to jump.

Exactly what her captors wanted.

After a month spent under their thumbs, she should know.

Uncertainty was the name of the game. Fear rode shotgun, stitching insecurity into her seams, needling down deep, right into her bones. The strategy was a good one. Diabolical. Cunning. Confusing as hell. She hadn't been mistreated or touched in ways she didn't want. Even enjoyed a certain amount of freedom inside the compound she shared with her fellow captives, but only at night.

A telling detail.

The men guarding her weren't around during the day. The prison went from active to quiet at five each morning, which was why she and the others got hustled back into their cells at 4:45 AM. Another turn in an already twisted game. More of the confusing push-pull. Allowed to roam free inside the common room, kitchen, gym and pool area without supervision, blocked from entering other areas by thick doors and tons of security. Good meals. Lots of books to read, games to play and crafts to tackle. Permitted to watch movies, but not the news. Zero computer or internet access. Which scared the crap out of her.

No matter how well the jerkoffs treated her, she had a bad, *bad* feeling. One Kasi, her one and only friend inside the prison, shared. The others might be oblivious, but she and Kasi *knew*. Something terrible awaited them. Something sinister. A *something* that left her wondering what the hell her jailers where planning.

A litany of possibilities plagued her. Night after night. Day after day. The running tally she kept inside her head never left her alone, throwing out one idea after another. The top three on her freak-the-hell-out list went something like:

One—sell her to highest bidder, a sexual sadist who'd get arrested in the real world if he did what he wanted to women behind closed doors. A serious possibility.

Two—use her for illegal science experiments. Already happened. At least, she thought it had. She didn't remember much about the night she'd been taken, but snatches of memory suggested she'd been in a medical suite of some kind. Combine that with the awful green drink they made her drink each night and...yup. Her Dr. Frankenstein theory held a lot of merit.

Three—the harvesting of vital organs for sick people on the black market. Again...the terrible tasting drink. Illegal organ donation might explain that odd detail.

Could be number one. Might be numbers two or three.

No matter how many times she asked, the guards gave nothing away. She always got the same response—silence. Which, of course, freaked her out even more, ramping fear into terror whenever she interacted with any of the men holding her against her will.

Grabbing one of the throw pillows propped against the headboard, Natalie plopped it in her lap. Fingers playing in the soft fringe, she wound the strands around her thumb and stared across the corridor. An almost identical cell sat opposite hers. Pale green walls instead of violet. White duvet on the bed with bright flowers instead of a light grey geometric pattern. Bigger armchair, same thick rug on the floor. Different girl staring back at her from behind glass across the aisle.

Blue eyes trained on her, Kasi mouthed, "Ready?"

Nerves tightened her throat. Natalie nodded anyway and mouthed back, "You?"

Kasi drew a deep breath. The end of her long, blonde ponytail swung as she tipped her chin.

"Go time."

Her friend's mouth curved. "Oorah."

The call sign Marines used made her want to laugh. Firing a warning look across the aisle, Natalie fisted her hands into the soft pillow, relegating her amusement to the back of her brain. She needed to focus and stay on point. It was almost time. The lockdown would lift soon, allowing her out of the gilded cage.

Natalie could hardly wait.

Kasi felt the same.

The intensity of her friend's stare told the tale, giving her eagerness away. An active girl, just like her, Kasi needed sports as much as she did to get rid of excess energy and the restlessness that always companied it.

She swam. Lap after lap in the Olympic-sized swimming pool.

Kasi climbed, using the enormous rock walls bracketing the pool area each night.

Time spent in close proximity had made them friends. Shared interests had done the rest, building the necessary trust needed to hatch the plan.

Tonight was the night.

Now or never.

After weeks of careful reconnaissance, she knew the cellblock by heart. Backwards. Forwards. The direction didn't matter. Having dyslexia might suck, but that didn't mean she was stupid. She thought in 3D, her mind functioning like few others did. Quick thinking and a photographic memory provided the rest, enabling her to remember things other people couldn't.

All she needed to do was see something once and...bingo. She held all information inside her head. The prison was no exception. She knew every camera location and angle and how the ventilation system worked. Memorized the code to the elevators by watching one of the guards punch it in. Possessed all the information she needed to slip under the radar and go unnoticed long enough to make out.

Nothing left to do now, but execute. Get the hell out and back to her life. Or rather...her new life. The old one, she knew, was over.

Not much of a loss, all things considered.

No family to miss. No friends on the outside to mourn. No real hardship in terms of leaving everything behind and picking up somewhere else.

Still, Natalie resented the necessity.

Her kidnappers had taken what didn't belong to them—her autonomy and freedom to choose, her right to life, liberty and the pursuit of happiness. So...

One way forward.

No retreat allowed.

Natalie exhaled long and smooth. No mistakes could be made. One misstep would trip the high-tech surveillance system, and the guys holding down the fort would sound the alarm. Give chase. Try to drag her back into her beautiful cage. Play hunting horseman to her running fox.

No way would she allow it to happen.

She'd waited weeks. Done her due diligence. Paid attention to tiny details, noticing the rhythms and patterns of activity inside the—

The air vent above her head activated.

Fresh air filtered into her room.

Her focus narrowed on the glass door. Any moment now. She counted off the seconds. In less than a minute, the airlock would pop and activate the motion detectors. Three. Two. One...

A click sounded.

Her cell door vibrated. The latch released. The clear panel slid sideways on an invisible track, opening a path to freedom.

Composed, not moving too fast, Natalie lifted the pillow from her lap and, setting it back against the headboard, waited for the telltale signs. The other girls exited their cells. She listened to the footfalls and soft greetings in the corridor as her fellow captives headed for open space and the common area.

Sliding toward the edge of the mattress, she listened harder. Deadbolts unlocked, soft clicking sounds falling like dominos as doors opened and closed. Taking her time, she plumped the pillow and rolled off the bed. Her bare feet touched down on the thick area rug. Anticipation running wild, so tense her muscles hurt, she stopped to pull on her socks and shoes.

Same actions. Different night.

A sequence she and Kasi had perfected over the last couple of weeks.

Everything needed to look normal. If she deviated from her usual routine, looked too eager, moved too fast, the guards would notice. She must hold the line. Do everything right. Make sure she didn't give whoever watched reason to linger on her longer than necessary.

With a controlled breath, she paused to straighten the homemade quilt lying across the foot of her bed. A gift. One she hadn't wanted, but couldn't deny she needed.

Well-loved by its previous owner, the worn softness soothed her. Smelled fresh and clean, like the seaside with a hint of wood smoke. She'd wrapped it around her more than once over the last few weeks, seeking comfort, needing something soft and warm to make her feel better about her imprisonment.

How he'd known she needed it, Natalie couldn't begin to guess.

Most nights she didn't want to either. Thinking about Hamersveld—and the kindness he showed her—was dangerous. The way she reacted to him bothered her.

She didn't like the guy.

Natalie pursed her lips as a small part of her protested. All right. Might as well be honest. She didn't dislike him either, but...well, she didn't *know* him. Not really. Beyond the gifts he left outside her door—the quilt and old-style iPod, a fancy hair brush, expensive soap and shampoo, warm slippers and flip-flops for her trips to the pool...the list went on and on—and yet, he'd only approached her twice. Once to say hello. The second time to ask if she needed anything.

Yes. Freedom. My life back.

Her growled grievance had made his eyes spark with humor.

She'd wanted to hit him. He'd backed away, and never returned.

He watched her, though...constantly. When she swam laps. When she listened to music or an audiobook poolside. While she sat in the common area with Kasi chatting, playing cards or watching TV. Or stood in the kitchen making a snack.

Always there. Forever around. In her orbit without being intrusive.

He was maddening. Intriguing. A Viking marauder looking for the right time to strike.

Anticipation hummed through her every time she laid eyes on him.

And no wonder.

Big, blond and intense, Hamersveld was beautifully made. A woman would have to be blind, deaf and dumb not to notice. Normally not something she worried about. See the man, admire the beauty, move on. A great motto. One Natalie wished she could take to heart, 'cause despite her best efforts, his deep voice and gentle way of speaking to her burrowed under her skin, making it impossible to ignore him.

Or deny the truth.

She was attracted to him. Seriously, off the charts *attracted*. The intensity of it startled her. The mere idea it existed at all freaked out her.

He was one of the bad guys.

She was one of the captured girls.

No way should she be wondering about him. Losing sleep over him. Wanting to get close just to see what happened. Her fascination with him was twisted. Wrong. A mistake. Hazardous to her health and yet...

And yet...

And yet...

Something about him grabbed her attention and held it. Which meant she needed to get with the program and put her plan into motion. Right now. Before he showed up and she lost her edge, along with the focus she needed to make sure the escape went off without a hitch and she and Kasi made it out alive.

3

Cranking the door open, Hamersveld stalked over the threshold into the bunker. Rusty hinges squawked behind him. No one noticed. Absorbed in the fight, males stood with teeth bared and fists raised. Anger clogging the air, nine warriors encircled three others, jeering at the trio, noses out of joint about something. Judging by the destruction—dents in corrugated steel walls, broken furniture scattered across the concrete floor, the amount of blood flowing—it wasn't difficult to guess what that *something* entailed.

Boots planted just inside the door, Hamersveld sighed.

Fucking Azrad.

The male was a pain in his ass. And destructive as hell.

Though, he couldn't help but admire the male's technique.

Movements fluid, Azrad and his shadows—Terranon and Kilmar—worked as a unit, standing back-to-back, moving in concert, delivering a beat down the likes of which he couldn't help but enjoy. Outnumbered, Azrad and his buddies should've been on the floor by now. Bloodied. Bruised. With remorseful attitudes and a shitload of broken bones. Instead, the triad dominated, taking on all comers, making their brothers-in-arms bleed.

Spinning beneath a punch, Azrad delivered another blow. Knuckles cracked against bone. The male grunted. Azrad whirled and, nailing one male with an elbow to the temple, unwrapped an uppercut beneath another's chin. The warrior's head snapped back. He folded, listing sideways toward the floor. Before he collided with concrete, Azrad lashed out with his foot, kicking the male coming to his friend's aid in the face. Blood arced through the air, splattering the wall as Azrad went after the downed Razorback.

Impressive.

Annoying.

Beyond dangerous.

He needed to stop to the squabble. Immediately. Before the warriors challenging Azrad ended up dead instead of injured. The prickly SOB only had so much patience. And given the intensity of the fight, he'd already lost what little he possessed. Now, all Azrad saw was red. Hamersveld read it in his body language. Saw it in his set expression. Felt it as powerful magic spiraled, cracking against metal, bending the walls outward, making the remaining Razorbacks scatter.

"Azrad," he yelled, walking toward the male.

His warrior didn't acknowledge his call. In full battle mode, he was too busy beating his opponent unconscious to care that his commander hailed him. He was too far gone. Teeth bared. Fists and dragon blood flying. Death in his dark blue eyes.

With a curse, Hamersveld unleashed his magic. A cyclone churned across the floor. A flurry of curses rose as males ran for cover. Water rose like a cobra behind Azrad, then struck. Salty fangs sinking deep, the magical serpent wrapped its coiled length around the warrior and dragged him away from the injured male.

The Razorback on the floor moaned.

Azrad snarled.

Hamersveld tightened his grip, holding the male down, shoving water down his throat until he sputtered, struggling to breathe. Flat on his back, pinned to the floor, water serpent rising about him, Azrad met his gaze. Magic powered up, threatening to go apocalyptic. The air around the male heated. Water steamed, turning to mist as glowing indigo eyes flashed in warning.

"Calm the fuck down," Hamersveld said, issuing an ultimatum of his own.

Terranon moved to help his friend. "Release him, Sveld."

"When he settles down."

Kilmar sidestepped and, hands flexing, approached him from the side.

Hamersveld growled at the male. Terranon was bad enough, but he didn't want Kilmar anywhere near him. An acid dragon, Kilmar was almost as powerful as Azrad. The warrior was toxic, one hundred percent deadly, commanding *Scald*—an exhale in dragon form comprised of natural napalm, acid and neurotoxins that took opponents apart scale-by-scale, then ate them alive. A true threat if the brutal SOB decided to enter the fray.

"Back off, Kilmar." Feet planted, shoulders squared, he glared at him from beneath his brows, asserting control, backing up his command. "I'm not hurting him."

"Fuck," Azrad said, looking as pissed off as he sounded. "KK, don't. I'm good. Let go, Sveld."

He scanned Azrad's face. Looked him in the eye. The raging glow in his warrior's eyes downgraded to a shimmer. Exhaling long and slow, he relaxed and... thank Silfer. Crisis averted. The male was back in control. Back inside his own skull, instead of nothing but rage and adrenaline.

Rewarding the change in attitude, Hamersveld recalled his magic. The snake evaporated, releasing its chokehold on Azrad. Water returned to him, rivulets slithering over steel walls, dropping from the ceiling, skating across the floor to reach him.

With a hum, he absorbed the H2O and eyed Azrad. "What the hell, whelp? I can't trust you for an instant, can I?"

Adjusting his black eye patch, Terranon growled. "The assholes started it."

"They always do." Grabbing a downed chair, Kilmar set it back on its feet.

"What are you two—five years old?" Palm planted on concrete, Azrad rolled to his feet.

A nasty gleam in his pale yellow-green eyes, Kilmar flipped his friend the bird.

Terranon laughed. "Don't know about you, but I like the smell of blood in the evening."

Azrad grinned.

Enjoying the byplay but refusing to show it, Hamersveld frowned. "Pains in my ass. All of you."

Slicking wet hair away from his face, Azrad shrugged. "Boredom breeds discontentment."

True enough.

Which meant it was past time to end the dragon combat competition. He needed to reshuffle his warriors and get everyone back out into open air. Keeping so many Razorbacks in the same lair—in such close quarters day after day, far from Seattle and the females who called the city home—was a recipe for disaster. The fact Azrad and his cohorts hadn't killed anyone over the last month was a miracle. Something to celebrate while he reassigned members of his pack to new locations.

His attention drifted to the gaggle of Razorbacks standing a safe distance away.

He clenched his teeth.

Fucking cowards.

Even at three to one odds, the males Rodin sent each month to fill Razorback ranks hadn't been able to best the trio gathered around him. Nothing but fledging warriors. Little combat experience. Zero brains. Nowhere near skilled enough to take on Bastian and his band of bastards each night. They needed more attention and training. Much more than he, as first-in-command, could provide by himself.

"Deal with him," he said to the frontrunner in the gaggle, pointing to the unconscious Razorback spread like a broken starfish on concrete. Flicking his fingers, he spoke to the warriors surrounding him. "You three —come with me."

Without waiting to see if the trio obeyed, he turned and walked away. Footfalls echoing across the hangar, he entered a narrow corridor that fed into a spiral staircase. Pace steady, boot soles clanking against steel treads, he descended into the belly of the beast. Built as a bomb shelter in WWII, the bunker boasted six main spaces—nuclear fallout shelter, mess hall, lounge and three large rooms with rows of army bunk beds. Azrad and his buddies staked out one, leaving the rest of the regiment to fend for themselves.

Battle lines had been drawn fast.

The instant warriors realized what the competition meant—the opportunity to breed one of Ivar's high-energy females—the infighting began. Touching an HE was a once in a lifetime opportunity. One a smart male knew not to take for granted. Plugged directly in the Meridian, HEs were rare. Beautiful, powerful, able to feed a male until he was full. Almost unheard of among his kind, so naturally, the competition was fierce. For more than just the obvious reasons.

Getting close to a high-energy female was incentive enough. Add in the chance for a warrior to impress Ivar and...boom. The fight went from sporting to gladiatorial.

Not surprising.

Good things happened to males Ivar favored.

He should know. The instant Ivar accepted him, his life changed for the better. Evened out. Provided him a purpose, allowing him to grow into a new skillset—the role of first-in-command. A position Hamersveld never would've believed himself capable of until he met Ivar.

Now he knew better.

He excelled at leadership. The more responsibility Ivar gave him, the more he thrived, becoming someone others looked to for answers. Which led to respect and camaraderie, the kind he'd never experienced and knew never to take for granted.

Reaching the bottom of the stairs, Hamersveld strode down the main corridor. The smell of must and damp kicked up. Ignoring peeling paint, rusty metal walls and bare light bulbs, he headed for the end of the hall and a wide steel door.

An office of sorts. His private space. A room without a view.

He issued a mental command. The keypad installed beside the door lit up. Beeping sounded as he punched the code in with his mind. The deadbolts flipped open. Listening to the heavy thud of footfalls behind him, he shoved the steel door open and stepped over the threshold. Habit made him scan the space as he walked past the ratty couch, giving Azrad and the gang enough room to enter behind him.

Skirting a couple of office chairs, he stopped in front of a large desk. Standard issue army fare. Metal. Utilitarian. Painted an ugly grey-green, leather blotter set on top. Not that he cared. He didn't spend a lot of time in the Cascades, preferring the comfort of the city lair to the shithole he presently stood inside.

"Sit," he said, waving his hand toward the sitting area.

Male muscle shuffled as Azrad set up shop. Planting himself on the back of the couch, he set his combat boots on the seat cushions. Dust puffed up as, arms crossed, Kilmar leaned against the wall by the door and Terranon kicked back in a faded wingback.

Blue-black hair gleaming in the low light, forearms resting on the tops of his spread thighs, Azrad leaned forward. Relaxed posture. Tattoo on display. Indigo eyes steady on him.

Hamersveld stared at the male's ink a second. Freaky as hell. More than a little off-putting, a red spider sat in the center of a black web inked into the side of his neck. Looked real, almost life-like, making him wonder if the spider in the web came alive (like Fen). Was the marking magic-driven? Or nothing but lines drawn on skin by human hands?

Good question.

No way of knowing, given Azrad refused to talk about it. Closed-mouthed most of the tine, no one but the warriors closest to him knew anything about the male, never mind his tattoo.

Hamersveld almost asked, then let his curiosity go. He didn't care that much. Azrad could keep his secrets as long as he got what he needed out of the warrior in the end.

Settling in, he leaned back against the edge of his desk and met Azrad's gaze. "The competition is over. The three of you are in."

Kilmar growled, eagerness in the undertone.

"Fucking A," Terranon murmured. "About time."

One corner of Azrad's mouth kicked up. "When do we meet them?"

"Who chooses first?" Terranon asked at the same time, talking over his leader.

"Azrad," Hamersveld said, eyeballing the three. "He's earned the right. You and Kilmar hold the two and three spots."

Kilmar raised a dark blond brow. "And if we both want the same female?"

Terranon rolled his unpatched eye.

"Draw straws. Fight it out." Gaze moving between the three, he shrugged. "I don't give a shit. Just as long as you're primed and ready to go when the Meridian realigns."

"We'll be ready," Azrad murmured, a strange, almost wary look in his eyes. "Who falls in the four, five and six spots?"

The question made Hamersveld tense, reminding him he still had a decision to make. Claim Natalie for himself or take her off the breeding program board entirely. Another excellent question, one he shoved to the side. He didn't have time to deal with his need for her now. Not while standing in front of three males with too much brain matter and the wherewithal to use it.

"Ivar and I will decide who will breed the remaining HEs in the coming days." Letting go of his grip on the metal edge, he pushed away from the desk. "In the meantime, the others stay here while you three head back to the city."

Terranon snorted. "Afraid we'll kill them all?"

Good guess. The most likely outcome if he left Azrad to his own devices. "Or I'm afraid I'll lose my temper and drown you in a puddle."

"Might want to do that now and save me the trouble," Kilmar said, glancing at Terranon.

"Aw, come on, KK. Don't be that way." An unholy glint in his good eye, Terranon grinned. "You know you love me."

"Hell," the male grumbled, making Azrad laugh.

Hamersveld's lips twitched. "You got a place to stay in town?"

"Yeah. All set." Plugging him with an intense look, Azrad hopped off the back of the couch. "When do we meet the HEs?"

"Two weeks."

Azrad frowned, causing the black metal stud piercing his eyebrow to shift against his skin. "We only get a week with our females before the realignment?"

"How much more time do you need?"

"With an HE? Every single second." Unusual yellow-green gaze leveled on him, Kilmar shifted his shoulders against the wall. "I want all three weeks."

Hamersveld grunted. He didn't blame the male. Given a choice, he wanted that, and more, with Natalie. "I'll take it under advisement. Let you know in a day or two. Now, move your asses. I want you gone before I speak to the others."

Tipping his chin, Azrad flicked his fingers in salute and made for the door. The second the trio left his office, Hamersveld bowed his head. Taut muscles screamed in protest. Holding the stretching, he absorbed the pain and, listening to the thump of fading footfalls, exhaled to break the tension. Three down, three more to choose if he didn't—

Static broke his train of thought, blasting through mind-speak. *"Sveld."*

He righted his head. *"What is it, Rampart?"*

"Your female's gone AWOL."

His female. The words hit him like a body shot. Sucking in a breath, Hamersveld shook his head. *"What?"*

"Natalie. The clever one," Rampart growled. *"She's on the run."*

Already out the door, Hamersveld sprinted down the corridor. *"How far has she gotten?"*

"Pretty far. She's—fuck. She's past the inner doors, heading for the service elevator. Is messing with the..." The fast click of computer keys came through the cosmic link, scoring his temples. *"Shit, Sveld. I know you don't want anyone touching her, but—"*

"Hands off, Ram. I'll be there in less than ten."

"Might be too late."

"Track her. Hack into human CCTV, use the street cams we set up if you have to, but—"

"Got it. I'll ping you if anything changes."

"Keep it on the down low. No one else in the loop."

Silence met his pronouncement.

"Ram," he growled, needing to protect a female he shouldn't, but already thought of as his own.

"For now. Things get out of hand, I gotta tell Ivar."

Charging up the stairs, Hamersveld severed the connection. The work of seconds, and he was aboveground, across the hangar, and through the front doors. The instant he cleared the metal structure, he shifted into dragon form and took flight. Cold blasted over his scales. Sitting outside keeping watch, Fen screeched and, following his lead, launched skyward.

Magic warped around him.

Fen on his wingtip, Hamersveld rocketed over the forest, toward 28 Walton Street, the lair he shared with Ivar and his personal guard.

No time to waste.

Natalie was out of pocket and heading for a fall. If he didn't lock her down, Ivar would. The male might love him—might even be amused by his decree no one go near Natalie—but that wouldn't keep him from protecting the integrity of the breeding program. His commander was on a mission. One designed to save all of Dragonkind. Little room for error. No tolerance for insubordination. Zero patience in the face of jail-breaks and obstinate females, so...yeah. No question. He needed to reach her first. Reach her fast. Before Rampart roused Ivar, and Natalie received a lesson no female wanted to learn.

4

Heart beating like runaway freight train, Natalie walked out of her cell into the central corridor. She met Kasi in the middle and turned right, toward the doors that would take her out of the cellblock. Already out of lockdown, the other girls walked toward the common area, faint slap of flip-flops lying down a soundtrack, giving her a locational grid. Well ahead of her. Passing beneath the archway leading into the combination living, dining and game rooms.

She listened harder. The soft drift of voices, then...

Nothing.

Blessed silence as the four others left the main hallway.

Almost to the wide steel door, she glanced sideways.

Kasi picked up the thread, starting the pre-planned conversation. "Swimming tonight, Nat?"

"I was going to, but..." Natalie paused, then shook her head. Playing it up for the cameras—and whoever sat in the command center watching them—she rubbed her shoulder. "Not tonight. My shoulder's sore."

Her friend quirked a brow. "Strain it last night?"

"Old injury. Too many laps. Front crawl's been bugging me lately."

"Sauna, then?"

Massaging the muscles between her shoulder and neck, she faked a grimace. "Yup. You wanna join?"

"You know what..." Kasi shrugged as she filed through the now open door, the one kept locked during the day. "I think I might. Gonna grab a bottle of water first, though. Want one?"

"If you don't mind. Can you grab me a power bar too?"

"No problem," Kasi said, peeling off, walking beneath the archway into the common area. Her destination? The mini-fridge stocked with bottles of water and energy drinks tucked beneath the bar at the back of the room. More routine. Same old, same old. Another box ticked off. She and Kasi always brought snacks into the pool area. All the better to protein-up after a steady swim and hard climb on the rock wall. "Meet you in the locker room."

"Sounds good," she said, tone even and light, keeping it casual to avoid raising suspicion.

A necessary game.

The jackoffs guarding the underground complex watched them like hawks.

Dragging her gaze from her retreating friend, Natalie scanned the open concept room beyond the archway. Her mind took a snapshot. Her memory supplied the rest. Huge space. Pale walls. Twenty-foot ceilings with enormous hurricane lamps hanging at even intervals over a series of deep-seated couches, wide-backed armchairs, and colorful beanbag footrests. Thick area rugs. Large nature prints on the walls. Built-in bookshelves with every game under the sun.

A honey colored table with eight dining chairs completed the picture, setting up shop in front of the marble topped bar against the back wall.

A comfortable space.

An ordinary looking room.

Another huge lie.

Nothing about the complex felt comfortable. A prison, after all, was a *prison*, no matter how fashion forward. No getting around the truth. She was a kidnap victim—a survivor—not a willing participant in whatever twisted game her captors played.

Continuing down the hall, Natalie came to another set of doors. She grabbed the handle and pushed. A click sounded. The heavy panel swung out. A second later, the scent of saltwater hit her. She breathed deep, drawing it into her lungs, letting the familiar smell work on her tension. Muscles knotted by stress unraveled. She sighed in reaction. Man, that felt good, like the promise of open water, starry skies and freedom, making her imagine she was home. In her tiny apartment overlooking Puget Sound.

A lovely mindscape.

A worthy thing to picture each day. Like postcards, her mind supplied a steady stream of distraction, helping her through active nights and quiet days. Water was her touchstone. A safe place. Her sanctuary whenever the world and its expectations became too much.

Lake. River. Open seas. The location didn't matter. The second her parents put her in a pool as a child, she found her bliss.

Natalie remembered every second of that day, even though she shouldn't. Most people didn't recall what happened to them at eleven months old, but she did—

vividly. The ripple and roll. The thrill of buoyancy. The warm, weighted comfort as she floated in endless drift.

She'd been swimming ever since. First for fun, later in competitions.

Swim meets had dominated her childhood, providing what he parents couldn't—stability, a sense of belonging, a safe place far from the screaming and yelling, from the violence of two people who claimed to love each other, but were really just out of control. And then finally, what they couldn't afford, a scholarship to one of the most competitive colleges around.

Not that it had done her much good.

Sure, she could swim. Blow the competition out of the water. Break records too. Problem was—she couldn't read. At least, not very well. Recall spun her around, then turned her inside out. All the recriminations from dysfunctional, but accomplished parents steeped in academic accolades. The humiliating talks with her coaches, and eventually the Dean. The inevitable loss of her scholarship.

Natalie clenched her teeth.

Dyslexia...the gift that just kept on giving.

Plagued by memories, she swallowed the sorrow and shut down the hurt. Mourning something never meant to be wasn't smart. Not right now, and as she crossed the threshold into the locker room, leaving the cameras and prying eyes behind, Natalie forced her mind away from the past into the here and now. She must stick to the plan and stay on task.

Time wasn't on her side.

Twenty minutes—half an hour tops—and the guards would come check on her. The jackoffs were nothing if not efficient...and predictable. A fact that worked in her favor. Well that, and good fortune. Cameras weren't installed in the locker room. None in the private bathrooms either.

A nod to a woman's modesty, no doubt.

Her captors were trying to be polite.

Their first big mistake. One she planned to exploit.

Half an hour might not be optimal, but she could work with it. She'd gone over and over the plan inside her head. Timed each phase. Smoothed out every wrinkle. Planned her escape down to the second, so if everything panned out, she and Kasi needed fifteen minutes. Just *fifteen minutes* to reach ground level and disappear.

Minutes after that, she'd be inside someone's house calling the police. She might not know the other women well, but she refused to leave them behind. The kidnapping ring—or whatever the hell it was—needed to be exposed, and the guards charged. Before another woman got shoved into one of the unoccupied prison cells.

Glancing over her shoulder, Natalie upped her pace.

On her toes, footfalls quiet, she ran past fancy benches between rows of wooden lockers. Very country club. Dark stained cabinetry, fancy black and white mosaic tiles, brushed nickel faucets, marble countertops, private showers...the best money could buy.

She rushed by a bank of sinks, then slid to a stop. Reaching under the last one, she felt for the screwdriver she'd hidden beneath the lip. Pilfered from an abandoned tool belt in the pool area, Natalie had taken it out of reflex. She hadn't known what she would use it for until she'd watched a work crew put in the final fittings in the locker room last week.

A happy accident.

One that allowed her to see the final piece of drywall being installed. The finishing touches didn't interest her. What lay beyond plaster and paint, however, did—a two-foot gap between the concrete outer wall and the metal stud inner wall. A narrow slice of space. Just room enough for her to slip between the foundation and wall running parallel to the main hallway.

The gap was a godsend. A way to bypass the security system, hide from cameras, and move around locked doors undetected. A dark tunnel that would funnel her toward the elevator at the end of the corridor her captors used all the time.

One she wasn't permitted to enter.

A death grip on the screwdriver, Natalie detoured to the sauna and, on the fly-by, cranked the dial. Red lights lit the controls as the cedar booth went active, heating in preparation for use. A precaution. Unnecessary? Maybe, but she needed to hedge her bets. If the sauna's system connected to the command center, she didn't want the man monitoring its sensors to think she wasn't in the locker room.

She stopped in front of a section of wall between the main room and shower area. Smooth plaster. Recent paint job. An unblemished white expanse. Raising the screwdriver, she drove the end into the drywall. The sharp tip punched through. She yanked it out and hammered the wall again. Dust clouds rose around her as she repeated the process, stabbing the wall over and over, creating a rectangular of small of holes.

Footsteps sounded behind her.

Whirling around, Natalie raised the screwdriver like a knife.

"Just me," Kasi whispered, fingers curled around two water bottles, hands up in self-defense, pockets of her hoodie stuffed full of power bars. Her friend pointed to the wall. "How we doing?"

"Almost through." Breathing hard, covered in drywall dust, wielding the screwdriver like a maniac, she made the last few holes. "Stand back."

Kasi nodded.

Natalie backed up and—

Bam!

Her foot punched through the wall. Hushed noise ricocheted, bouncing off hard tile. Anxiety curled through her. She kicked the wall again. The section between the little holes dimpled, then folded inward. Using her hand, Natalie shoved through the drywall into empty space beyond. She took a moment to look, to make sure her calculations were right. No impediments. Little debris. Nothing but clear sailing, a straight shot past the locked doors in the corridor.

Looking over her shoulder, she met Kasi's gaze. "One more thing."

"What?"

"If I get caught, and you have a chance—"

"I'm not leaving you behind."

"Kasi."

This girl. So brave. Ridiculously loyal. Especially given the short amount of time they'd known each other. Then again, Natalie guessed prison did that to people. Knit friendships together, binding hearts and minds tight.

In another life, she and Kasi would've been fast friends. Common interests and a true liking for one another would've turned into something more. Something greater—lattes and Saturday afternoons spent shopping, road trips, laughter and secrets shared. Instead, they had *this*...a screwed-up pact that meant leaving her friend behind if things went from crappy to critical.

Regret welling inside her, Natalie abandoned the argument and, shoving the screwdriver in her pocket, crawled through the hole. Her feet touched down on the other side. Concrete rasping beneath her shoe soles, she helped Kasi climb over the lip, then spun into the gap. Senses pricked, staying as quiet as possible, Natalie picked her way around metal studs, heading into dense shadows.

Running the gauntlet, she reached the end of the tunnel. Muscles tense, heart hammering, praying hard, she pressed her ear to the wall. Mostly quiet. No voices or footfalls coming from the other side. Just a low humming sound.

A repeat with the screwdriver.

Another series of small holes.

Using her knee and shoulder, Natalie broke through the other side into...

"Thank God," she whispered, staring into the depths of a utility room.

A terrific bit of luck.

The enclosed room full of mechanical equipment provided cover. Enough to get her bearings. Scanning the space, she climbed over the hip high edge. A furnace and air exchanger sat off to the side. A few generators chugged along opposite her, energy efficient engines rumbling above any sounds she made.

Another stroke of unexpected luck.

All she needed to do now was hope fortune stayed with her. Long enough for her to find her way free.

Listening to Kasi behind her, she crossed to the

door. Crouched to one side, she held her breath, turned the handle, then exhaled in relief. No lock. Moving slowly, she cracked the door open and peered down the hallway. Shiny elevator doors glinted in the low light, taunting her, reassuring her, making hope rise hard.

Her eyes strayed to the electronic keypad.

Locking her muscles, Natalie quelled the urge to sprint toward freedom. She stayed still instead, forcing herself to be smart, and opened the utility room door wider. Just enough for her to peer in the other direction.

Locked double doors thirty feet away.

Camera pointed at it.

Nobody around.

With her index finger pressed to her lips, she signaled for Kasi to be quiet and inched into the corridor. Her friend on her heels, she slid along the wall and, staying low, headed for the elevator, hoping the code hadn't changed in the last twelve hours. Getting into the elevator was their only chance. The second the doors opened and closed behind them, she and Kasi's odds went up.

Way, way up.

Reaching the elevator, she made quick work of punching in the code. As the electronic keypad activated, beeping with each number she hit, she started to pray. To God. To the universe. To anyone who would listen.

"Please, please, please," she murmured as Kasi crouched beside her.

She pressed in the last two numbers.

Nothing happened.

"Shit," Kasi whispered, panic in her tone and—

A hum broke through the buzz of boxy fluorescent lights.

The elevator doors slid open.

Grabbing her hand, Kasi pulled her into the steel box and turned to the control panel. Two options—one button with an arrow pointing up, the other with the arrow pointing down.

Kasi hammered the up button, holding it down.

The door closed. Gears ground into motion.

Natalie almost sobbed in relief. She turned to Kasi instead and, gripping her upper arms, launched into the discussion she didn't want to start. They needed to get a few things straight. It needed to be said. Must be understood and—

Kasi shook her head. "Don't say it."

"I have to. You know I do. We need to be prepared for anything," she said, giving her friend a gentle shake, ignoring her pissed off look as the elevator ascended in a fast, smooth glide. "One of us needs to make it out of here alive. I hope we both get out, but neither of us knows what's on the other side of these doors. If the worst happens, and one of us gets caught, the other must do what's necessary. No matter how difficult."

"Goddamn it, Nat."

"If it's me, you run, Kasi. Don't think. Don't second-guess, just run. Get somewhere safe. Call the police."

"I can't believe you're sugg—"

"Promise me," she said, the words coming hard. "Promise me, Kasi. If I get caught, you'll do what I ask and *run*."

Tears swimming in her eyes, Kasi flexed her hands. "I hate this."

"I know."

"It shouldn't be either or."

"But it might be, so—"

"I promise." Expression tight, an unhappy light in her eyes, Kasi broke her grip. An instant later, she was in her friend's arms, wrapped in a fierce hug. "I know we don't know each other all that well, but...I love you, Nat. You're the best."

"Love you too," she whispered, her chest so tight it hurt to breath. "Remember—whatever happens, stay safe. Nothing familiar for a while. You get low and stay that way. Take care of yourself."

The elevator floor dipped, then settled.

Kasi let her go.

A ping sounded as the doors slide to the side.

Not wasting as second, Natalie raced over the threshold. The smell of paint thinner hit her. Her brain provided a quick snapshot. White plaster patches on grey drywall. An expanse of raw, unvarnished wood floor underfoot. Wide bank of cracked windows along the far wall. Elevated view into a backyard full of rusty oil tanks and construction equipment. From the angle and sightline, she knew instantly she was on the third floor of an old building.

Her focus snapped left.

Concrete staircase leading down. The thump of heavy footfalls echoed through the quiet, coming from around a blind corner to her right and—

"What the hell?" a guy growled. Thick German accent. Pitch black gaze set in an angular face. Expression shifting from surprised to furious. Feet planted shoulder-width apart, a nasty glint entered his eyes gaze as he cracked his knuckles. "Female, you're in for it now. Stop and turn around...or learn a lesson you won't soon forget."

Terror streaked through her.

Adrenaline hit her like rocket fuel, turning her legs into pistons as she shoved Kasi ahead of her and sprinted for the stairs, praying she made it out before the guy chased her down and dragged her back into hell.

5

W hite contrails streaming off his wingtips, Hamersveld rocketed out of thick storm clouds. Woodland gave way to pinpricks of light as the sky above him faded and the city came into view. Wind whistled over his horns, rattled his scales, then whipped off the jagged tip of his tail. His sonar pinged. He scanned the landscape below. Small rows of houses sitting on narrow boulevards leveled up into apartment high-rises, then streamed into wide boulevards fronting expensive homes in a more affluent neighborhood.

Almost there.

Just minutes away.

Banking away from downtown, Hamersveld flew west, over waterways and bridges. Big city turned into suburbs. Blasting over homes full of sleeping humans, he fired up mind-speak.

Static spiraled through time and space. The connection caught. He pinged his warrior. *"Status report."*

A crackling hiss raked his temples. Heavy footfalls echoed through the cosmic line as Rampart linked in. *"I'm mobile."*

Hamersveld bared his fangs. *Hristos.* Bad news. If Rampart was on the move, Natalie had made it out of the underground lair. Ingenious little water lily. If he wasn't so worried about her welfare, he'd have been proud of her.

"Where is she?"

"Game room, topside. Blondie's with her. And..."

The pause drew Hamersveld tight. Nothing good rested in what his friend didn't want to say. *"What?"*

"Denzeil."

"Shit. You tell him—"

"I did," Rampart growled. *"You know what he's like."*

"I'm going to kill him."

"Sveld, ping him. He might back off if you—"

"Like hell. The fucker hates me."

Not surprising, given Ivar refused him the title, naming Hamersveld first-in-command instead of Denzeil. The male's nose had been out of joint ever since. The idiot wouldn't even talk to him, making life more difficult than it needed to be.

Ivar kept asking him to be patient.

Hamersveld tried. All the damn time. Going against his own nature, he leashed his temper night after night, determined to lead by example instead of ripping D's head off. But if Denzeil continued his defiance—if he touched Natalie, marked her even a little —all bets would be off. Comrade or not, he'd gut the male, and not give it second thought.

An elevator dinged, echoing through mind-speak.

Boot soles slid across concrete. *"How far out are you, Sveld?"*

Hamersveld checked his trajectory. Night vision pinpoint sharp, he spotted his target. Three story brick building dead ahead. Backyard littered with rusty oil tanks and ancient construction equipment, 28 Walton Street—the 1930s firehouse he shared with the command unit of the Razorback pack—stood less than a mile away. *"Twenty seconds."*

"Good, cuz D's not answering me."

Figured.

Denzeil wouldn't pass up the chance to mess with him. Or hurt a female under his protection. The male's hatred ran too deep. At first, he'd agreed with Ivar—give Denzeil enough time, and he'd come around. Now, Hamersveld no longer cared. He was done. Done with the bullshit. Done being patient. Done with the disrespect.

Eyes on the firehouse, wings spread wide, Hamersveld blasted over the trees surrounding the property. Evergreens bowed beneath him, tops whipping forward before snapping back. Pine needles blew sky high, pinging off his scales as he jetted out of the woods. The storm he dragged in his wake rolled into the backyard. A front-end loader left the ground, flipped sideways, smashing into a row of bulldozers.

Steel shrieked.

Rubber tires whined.

The scent of leaking fuel infused the air.

Ignoring the calamity, Hamersveld scanned the rear of the building. Pitted brick façade. Narrow balconies. Wall-to-wall windows, three sets of French doors. Soft light glowed behind the cracked panes on the top floor, providing a clear view into the large room running along the back of the firehouse.

He focused on the windows and—

Hamersveld growled as he spotted his female. Sea-green aura flaring like a supernova, long ponytail streaming behind her, Natalie ran for the stairs. Breathing hard, her chest rose and fell as she glanced over her shoulder. He tapped into her bioenergy. Not that he needed to read her to know what she felt. The bright burn of her aura told him all he needed to know. She was terrified, scrambling to stay ahead of the male chasing her across the room.

Gaining on her, Denzeil reached out. His hand clawed at her shoulder. Stumbling, Natalie fumbled for something inside her pocket. She pulled out a screwdriver and, with a vicious stroke, stabbed his hand. Metal scored his comrade's skin. D cursed, but didn't stop. Grabbing a fistful of her sweater, he jerked her backward.

She screamed.

Denzeil yanked again, wrenching her sideways.

As she lost her footing, the scent of her fear hit Hamersveld, ripping him apart.

Aggression streamed through the fissure, all of it focused on the warrior who should've known better. Should've adhered to the code and backed off. Gone into hands-off-follow-at-a-distance mode when he realized Natalie cracked the security measures. The instant Hamersveld staked his claim—given the order she wasn't to be touched—she'd gone from fair game to off limits.

In a heartbeat.

No exceptions.

Denzeil knew it. He just didn't care.

Magic frothing in front of him, Hamersveld issued a command. French doors blew open. Hinges groaned, then let go. Glass exploded as thick wooden panels cartwheeled into the firehouse. He steered the pair's course, aiming for Denzeil's head.

The male cursed. Throwing Natalie toward the wall, he dove sideways.

Streaking over the balcony, Hamersveld shifted,

moving from dragon to human form. Not bothering with clothes, he somersaulted through the hole in the wall. Sliding across the wooden floor on bare feet, he unleashed more magic. Thick streams of water reared like a multi-headed Hydra. Slithering like a sidewinder, the water serpent wrapped around Natalie, shielding her from harm as its coiled length dragged her to safety behind him.

She gasped in alarm.

Hamersveld ignored her reaction and raked her with his gaze. None the worse for wear. Frightened. Shocked. Staring at him as though he'd grown a second head, but no injuries he could see, and yet, he couldn't let it go. Couldn't forgive and forget. Refused to give Denzeil a free pass. Not this time.

Primal instinct morphed into unmatched brutality. He advanced. Denzeil retreated, scrambling toward the elevator doors. As the idiot looked for a way out, Hamersveld let his inner beast out to play. His dragon half wanted to drown the male. Force water into his mouth and down his throat. Fill his lungs full while Denzeil choked on his own vomit.

Hamersveld held the line, refusing to go that route. Drowning the warrior was too easy. Not vicious enough. Denzeil had touched Natalie. Put his filthy hands on her. Now, nothing less than tearing him apart would do. He needed to rip him limb from limb. Wanted the male's blood on his bare hands, smeared across his chest, streaming in warm rivulets down his legs to pool around his feet.

Snarling his intent, Hamersveld stalked him across the room.

With no route of escape, Denzeil raised his fists and prepared to fight.

Hamersveld hammered through his guard.

Knuckles slammed D's cheekbone. A crack echoed in the empty room. Enlivened by the sound, Hamersveld unleashed a right cross. Pain radiated up his arm. The asshole's head snapped to the side. Blood splattered across the wall. He hit him again. And again. Rage leading the way. Fists flying. Savagery unleashed in every brutal strike.

Countering, Denzeil tried to fight back.

Hamersveld showed no mercy, taking him apart one punch at a time.

Blood running down his face, Denzeil bared his teeth. "She's not yours, Sveld. You haven't fucked her. Haven't agreed to breed her. You have no claim."

Hamersveld didn't answer.

He attacked instead, driving the male headfirst into the wall. Newly installed drywall dented. Dust puffed around him as he turned his fists into battering rams. Injured, trying to save face, D swung wild. Dipping beneath the punch, Hamersveld hammered him in the ribs. Bone snapped. Denzeil sucked in a pain-filled breath. His knees buckled and—

The elevator doors opened.

His water serpent hissed.

"Fuck," Rampart growled as he crossed the threshold with Syndor and Midion on his heels. "Midion—retrieve the blonde. Syn—grab D."

With a nod, Syndor veered toward the fight.

Sprinting the other way, Midion made for the stairs and the front door three floors down.

One hand fisted in D's hair, the other raised to hit him again, Hamersveld snarled at his friend.

"Christ." Sliding to a stop, Rampart raised his hands. Palms up, he held them out to the sides. A non-threatening, don't-attack-me gesture. "I know he deserves it, Sveld, but you can't kill him. Ivar's forbidden it."

"Like I care?"

"Brother," his friend murmured, the understanding in his tone so pronounced Hamersveld wanted to tear his face off. Hazel-gold eyes shimmering, Rampant met his gaze. Calm, cool and collected. Unphased in the face of a water dragon's fury. "Let him go and see to your female."

Your female.

Hamersveld sucked in air tainted by the scent of dragon blood. His nostrils flared. Yes. *His.* Natalie was *his.* His to protect. His to touch. No one else owned the right.

With a growl, he let Denzeil go.

Unconscious, the male fell forward, hitting the floor with a thud as Hamersveld turned toward Natalie. Cradled by the snake, protected by his magic, she stared at him. Her mouth moved. No sound came out as shock spun her around the lip of insanity.

"I don't...I don't..." Swallowing hard, she shook head. "I don't understand. What...what...what are you?"

"Dragonkind, Natalie. Half human, half dragon, and from the second I first saw you, one hundred percent yours." Pace quick, gaze locked on her, he strode through the water, splashing through wet coils of the water snake. Big green eyes collided with his as he reached for her. She drew in a quick breath. He cupped her face with both hands. Heat throbbed through his veins as he held her in his palms. "Which makes you *mine.*"

"No," she whispered. "That can't be."

"But it is," he said, his lips a breath away from hers.

"Deep down, you know the truth. You feel it in your gut, the same way I do."

She shook her head.

He dipped his and invaded her mouth. The glory of her taste hit. Bliss whispered through him. Pleasure lashed him with its tail and...fucking hell. A month spent watching and wanting, going through the motions and to bed alone, suffering acute need and unending desire. He'd dreamed of having her, holding her, touching her from the moment he laid eyes on her.

Complete torture.

An utter waste of time.

Without conscience or mercy, Hamersveld kissed her the way he wanted. Long. Hard. Deep. And wet. Taking as she gave. Giving as Natalie took, her surging energy sending a clear message. She wanted him too. Desired his touch as much as he loved having her in his arms. Deepening the intimacy, he tangled his tongue with hers and accepted what she offered. The Meridian hummed as he linked in, opening the connection. She whimpered. He stoked her appetite, feeding her delight, drawing the energy he needed to stay healthy and strong out of her, into him and—

She moaned.

His body reacted, hardening so fast it hurt and... Goddess be good to him. She was amazing. Better than any female he'd ever touched. Beautiful and generous. Delicious and life affirming. All he wanted and everything he'd been missing. She tasted like a warm, stormy day at sea. Like freedom and promise, the cure for the loneliness that plagued him as she buried her hands in his hair and kissed him back.

Need burned through him.

Murmuring her name, he took her by storm, overwhelming her senses, glutting his own, feeding hard and fast. Natalie didn't fight him. She accepted and gave, gentling him little by little until the kiss turned languid and lazy.

A tangle of tongues.

A sharing of tastes.

Discovery at its best.

One arm wrapped around her, he cupped her face with his free hand and drew away. Eyes closed, she tipped her chin up, asking without words for more. He kissed her again. Softly. Slowly. Relishing the zip of her bioenergy as he held her in the palm of his hand. "Natalie."

Drunk on the effects of a fast feeding, her eyes opened. Unfocused green eyes met his. Auburn eyelashes flickered as she struggled to regain her equilibrium. "Yeah?"

"Wanna get out of here for a while?"

"Out of here?"

Water serpent entwined around them, Hamersveld drew her deeper into his arms. Cradling her against him, he brushed wet hair away from her face and allowed his gaze to wander. "Goddess, you're pretty."

Mind fuzzy and body resting against his, she blinked. A slow up and down. "What?"

"Never mind. Stay foggy, *shaleima*," he murmured, calling her water lily in Dragonese. The endearment suited her. She carried the sultry notes of summer and sweetness. Of lazy nights and sleepless days. "I have something I want to show you. It's beautiful. You'll like it there."

Her brow furrowed.

He kissed her again, strengthening the connection, heightening her pleasure, tasting her deep. Brushing his mouth against hers one more time, he gathered her up and pivoted toward the door. The water serpent followed, slithering into mini-cyclones, dancing around him before he recalled the magic. Water returned to him, evaporating as he stepped onto the narrow balcony.

A current of cold air hit him.

Natalie flinched.

Conjuring a spell, he murmured his wishes. Warmth spilled into the air around her, creating a protective bubble. She sighed. He kissed her again, enjoying the way she snuggled in, accepting his touch.

"Hold tight, Natalie," he murmured, trying to prepare her for the shift and what she would witness. Him in dragon form, her new position nestled in the center of his paw. "Don't be afraid. Know that I won't hurt you."

"Okay," she mumbled, eyes closed, still groggy, too relaxed to be concerned.

A circumstance subject to change.

Females never reacted well to the sight of a male in dragon form at first. Most freaked out before he calmed them down. Usually by mind-scrubbing his partner of the moment while he connected to the Meridian through her and fed. Better that way. Maximum pleasure without the hassle.

With Natalie, though, he didn't want to adjust her memory. He wanted her to know him. Accept him for who and what he was, not the normal male he pretended to be to get what he needed. Which meant he must throw out the rulebook and be honest. Go against instinct, and give her something he never gave females—the truth. Show her instead of shield her. A foreign concept, but as he shifted into dragon form, unfurled his wings and leapt skyward, he stayed true, allowing her to experience the fullness of him.

She sucked in a shocked breath.

Conjuring a cloaking spell, he soared into open skies and turned north. Toward his cabin by the lake. To his hideaway in the wilderness. Time to do what he wanted instead of what his new pack demanded. The threat of Ivar and certain exile be damned.

6

Bone deep relaxation lifted a layer at a time. Natalie floated in mental drift, content in the sway as Hamersveld carried her away. On some level, she knew it was happening. The weirdness was hard to miss, never mind ignore. Especially when instinct kept prodding her, warning she was making a mistake. One of epic proportions and indeterminable magnitude. And yet, self-preservation remained quiet. Absent instead of active, even though she understood, as far as challenges went, the Dragonkind angle was a big one.

A huge hurtle.

Another reason to rewrite the history books.

People needed to be told men with the ability to transform into dragons were living next door, wandering around Seattle unchecked, occupying open skies. Right under the noses of human authorities. Though, what any of them could do about a cohort of dragons was anyone's guess.

An outcome Natalie didn't want to contemplate.

Her brain didn't listen.

Clearing the mental blur a bit at a time, her imagination tossed out suggestions, freaking her out by listing all the possibilities. Ones that would no doubt involve big explosions and lots of death.

Clinging to the sway and drift, Natalie wished it all away. An unusual approach for her. She'd always been a straight shooter, a take the bull by the horns kind of girl, but with Hamersveld in full flight and her curled up inside a dragon paw—scaled talons and lethal-looking claws inches away—denial seemed like the best option.

Her mind refused to take the hint...again.

More scary possibilities streamed into her head.

Breathing deep, Natalie tried to stem the rising tide of alarm. Panicking never helped. She needed to stay calm, think things through, and regain her bearings. Not her physical one. No chance of that considering she didn't know where Hamersveld was going. He'd grabbed her, kissed her stupid, stolen her will to resist, and flown away. No time to object. Little chance to adjust. Zero to sky-high in one-point-five seconds, so...yeah. Clearing her mind, getting her mental bearings, sounded like a spectacular idea. The best, given she was screwed and in need of another plan.

A foolproof one.

Against a *dragon*.

Her heart tripped inside her chest, then stumbled, picking up a beat. As it hammered the inside of her chest, Natalie chewed on the inside of her lip, struggling to come up with a new strategy. Discarding one after another, she curled into a tighter ball as Hamersveld banked into a turn. Her stomach sloshed. Bile kicked into the back of her throat. She swallowed the burn and, battling to control her reaction, breathed in through her nose and out her mouth. Inhale to the count of four, exhale for two. Just...

Breathe.

Drawing more air into her lungs, she forced herself out of intellectual gridlock. Fear downgraded a little at a time. Her brain re-engaged. Mental acuity sharpened, dragging awareness in its wake, making her realize despite the crazy flight, she wasn't cold. She should've been. Wet clothes combined with winter air never equaled warm, but as she cracked her eye open—and got a load of Hamersveld in all his Dragonkind glory—Natalie realized something important. He was the one keeping the chill at bay...and also, that she wasn't afraid.

Not really.

Despite the lethal vibe—fangs, claws and scales—he didn't seem that scary to her.

She frowned. All right, so all the dragon stuff sparked an array of WTF, but putting that aside, she discovered the longer she stared up at him, peering between massive talons and sharp claws, the more she relaxed, becoming more herself and less unsure of him.

Weird.

Unexpected.

Crazy making.

Giving him the benefit of the doubt was a bad idea. Another in a long line of them for her. She shouldn't be lying passively in his paw. She ought to be struggling—screaming, snarling, treating him to the sharp edge of the temper. An excellent strategy. The perfect approach. One horrendous problem. She didn't want to yell at him. What she wanted to do was ask questions and get answers. Which meant...

She'd lost what little remained of her mind.

No other explanation needed. No understanding her fascination with Hamersveld either.

The second she saw him shift and somersault

through the blown-to-bits French doors, she'd been riveted, fascinated, fighting the urge to know more.

Frowning, she returned to the rundown, replaying the scene after she exited the elevator frame by frame, watching it unfold like a film inside her head. Hamersveld blasting over the balcony—wings spread wide, eyes aglow as he snarled at the other guy. His shift from monster to man. Oh, and let's not forget, the little dragon.

Lord help her.

Between the shock of seeing a dragon and the water snake coiled around her, she'd almost missed him. The entire time Hamersveld beat the snot out of his friend, the pint-sized dragon—scales the same color as Hamersveld's—sat on the balcony, head tilted, watching with rapt attention. Hamersveld, mostly. More than once, however, his yellow vertical slitted gaze shifted to her, and she swore the beast was thinking. Calculating the odds. Working out problems. Wondering who she was and what she meant to Hamersveld.

Until he told her—point blank.

No mistaking the meaning of his *mine*, or the heat in his kiss, but...

Natalie sucked in another breath. It wasn't possible. She didn't belong to him. The kiss had surprised her, that was all. Her reaction meant nothing. Was an anomaly best left forgotten and never repeated. Except...

She'd kissed him back.

Repeatedly.

Every time his mouth touched hers, she'd lost her mind, reacting with heat and longing...and a need so profound it embarrassed her. And wasn't that just a kick in the pants? Something else to rail about. Her desire for him needed to die a swift death. Otherwise, she'd end up giving him everything he wanted in an exchange so carnal, it could only end one way —with her wrapped around him, and him deep inside her.

Another bad idea.

Incomprehensible, considering—

"Almost there, Natalie."

Hamersveld's voice streamed into her head. Norwegian accent. Gorgeous baritone. Deep, dark, just the right amount of rumble as the words scraped the inside of her temples. Tingles attacked, rolling down her spine, caressing her skin, raising goose bumps.

Natalie jolted. "What are you doing?"

"Talking to you."

"How?" One word. Powerful question. She could *hear* and *understand* him without him speaking out loud. Her brows collided. "I just heard you inside my head."

"Normal for us now." He glanced down at her. Shimmering black eyes rimmed by a light blue met hers. *"We've touched. I've fed. The bond between us is incredibly strong, Natalie. Now, that it's active, I can talk to you through mind-speak."*

Despite the weirdness, curiosity got the better of her. "Mind-speak?"

"A cosmic connection my kind uses to communicate."

"Okay." Pursing her lips, she chewed on that tidbit for a moment. "If I wasn't freaked out before...and just to let you know, I was...I'm more freaked out now."

"No need."

"Easy for you to say. You're a dragon. You've got the upper hand."

His mouth curved, exposing a fang as steam puffed from his nostrils. Water droplets rained down, beading on the invisible barrier surrounding her. *"True, but I would sooner lose my horns than hurt you."*

Good to know. Excellent news given she lay curled inside his paw. "How does it work?"

"Mind-speak?"

"Yeah."

"Magical threads unspool to create cosmic connections." Angling his wings, he descended through heavy clouds, losing altitude. As he leveled out, she got her first look at the terrain. Jagged mountain range to her right. Huge trees down below. Slashes of moonlight sparkling off a lake in the distance. *"I knock on your mental door. If you accept, I link in and you hear my voice."*

"Guess I accepted."

"You did."

Crap. She hadn't meant to accept anything, which led to another thought. One more daunting than mental doors and magical links. "Can you read my mind?"

"Only if you let me."

"Don't hold your breath."

He huffed. The low chuckle sounded rusty, as though he hadn't used it in a while. The realization shook her awareness of him loose. Understanding streamed into the gap, and she knew—*knew* with a knowing no one normal should—that Hamersveld hardly ever laughed. He didn't know joy, understand spontaneity, or welcome new experiences. Any other time, she would've cried foul. Called her conclusion pure supposition, but as intuition lit the fuse, suspicion tumbled into certainty. He was a conundrum wrapped in a beautiful package. A puzzle in need of solving. Vicious with others, yet kind to her. More honest than she expected him to be. Maybe even a little bit honorable, which didn't make any sense.

He was part of a kidnapping ring.

How could he be that guy and still be gentle, patient, and protective with her?

Looking at him was like staring at a split screen—one half listing the pros, the other crammed full of cons. Dichotomy at its finest. Enough conflicting information to keep her both intrigued and guessing. The fact she wanted to know what made him tick muddied the water even further. Pencil in her attraction to him and everything went sideways—her mind, her body, along with everything she believed about herself.

She was a strong woman, self-assured and independent. She stood her ground and didn't tolerate men who treated her with anything less than respect.

Her interest in Hamersveld, however, pushed past boundaries, expanding her horizons.

The mystery of him—the allure of the forbidden—pulled curiosity out of the shadows, opening up new possibilities. None of which she understood, but even as she resisted the tug, Natalie sensed the connection. She felt its presence as the bond strengthened, making her wonder about things she shouldn't. Like how much she enjoyed hearing him laugh and liked the look and sound of him. He did something strange to her. Sparked something primal and possessive, forcing her to acknowledge things unseen.

Impossible dreams.

Treacherous illusions.

The idea took shape and form anyway, spinning her imagination in dangerous directions. Toward fairy tale endings with a man of her own. Someone to love and be loved by in return. A fantasy most women indulged in at some point or other, but that didn't mean it was rooted in reality. She was a big girl, wise in the ways of the world. Her parents taught her more about dysfunction than any one person needed to know, and happily-ever-after with a man-dragon? Natalie frowned. Well, that was pie in the sky stuff. Magical thinking. The worst sort of self-delusion.

She might be attracted to Hamersveld—he might enjoy indulging her—but that didn't make him safe.

Instinct threw down the warning.

Determined to be brave, Natalie picked up the gauntlet. "What are you going to do with me?"

"Make love to you, if you let me. Bathe you in pleasure while I please myself."

She drew in a sharp breath. In surprise or outrage, she didn't know. "Well, that's direct, at least."

"Only way I know how to be, shaleima. I won't lie to you."

"Ever?"

"Ever."

"Crap," she whispered, chewing on her thumb nail, trying to process the honesty, afraid of her own curiosity...and the direction it would send her. "You're not making it easy for me to dislike you."

He snorted in amusement.

Pleasure, shiny and bright, shivered through her, making desire run wild. She couldn't help it. His accent, the sound of his voice, made her think about his mouth. And thinking about his mouth turned her attention toward the softness of his lips. As inevitable as the rising sun, the rest of the dominoes fell, and she remembered—the taste of his kiss, the heat of his hands, the strength of his body and—

"Fuck," he growled. *"I can hear what you're thinking."*

"I doubt that," she said, forcing herself to think of

something else. Just in case. She didn't need him wandering down the naughty trail her brain kept taking her. "I haven't let you all the way in."

He laughed again. *"Something for me to work toward, then."*

"Why would you bother?"

He didn't answer.

She refused to let it go. "You kidnapped me, Hamersveld."

"Wasn't me, Natalie."

She frowned, trying to remember the night she'd been taken. Everything was a blur. Almost as though her mind had been airbrushed, the incident glossed over. She recalled coming out of the sports center after her swim. Remembered crossing the parking lot toward her car, then...nothing. No memory to speak of until she woke up in a strange bed, locked in a pretty room behind a glass wall.

"You weren't there?"

"No, baby," he murmured, voice full of regret. *"You and the others were taken without my knowledge. I never agreed to that devil's bargain."*

Relief rolled through her.

Crazy reaction. Completely out of step with how she ought to feel. Angry. Betrayed. Horrified. Something in his tone, however, arrested her mid-fury. His sincerity drove home the undeniable. Hamersveld disagreed with what had been done. Believed kidnapping women amounted to a *devil's bargain*. Disliked her imprisonment almost as much as she hated the inside of her cell. And yet...

She refused to let him off the hook.

Disagreement hadn't led to action. She'd been kept underground for a month. *A month.* And he hadn't done anything to set her free.

"Doesn't make you innocent of the crime. I was taken against my will. Held for—"

"*Twenty-seven days, eleven hours, and forty-three minutes.*"

She blinked. Holy crap. He'd kept track. Made inquiries about her. Knew exactly how long she'd been sitting in that prison cell.

The idea should've scared her, but as she stared up at him, her anger dried up. Hamersveld might not be blameless, but he had done something. He'd intervened. Made a statement of some kind. One that kept the guards from bothering her. A reason to be grateful. The other girls hadn't been so lucky.

Her throat went tight. The corners of her eyes started to sting.

Refusing to cry, Natalie shut down the waterworks. A hard thing to do, especially as gratefulness spilled into appreciation. She wanted to thank him. She wanted to reach out and touch him. She wanted to tell him how much she valued his protection. No matter how much she hated her prison cell, her time there could've been so much worse. She might have been battered, bruised and raped instead of simply held against her will...if not for Hamersveld.

"Thank you for warning them away."

"*Shaleima,*" he said, tone soothing, understanding in his eyes. "*No one touches you but me. I can't help the others, but you? You're mine. I made sure every male inside the lair knew it.*"

More reasons to be thankful. And maybe, a touch frustrated too.

She hadn't agreed to anything...yet. The idea she might made her go nine rounds inside her head. None of it made sense. Not her capture. Not her reaction to him. Not his insistence he could help her, but not keep Kasi and the others safe.

What the hell was going on?

A question she'd been asking for weeks, and as Hamersveld flew in low, gliding toward a town, she wondered if he meant what he said. Would he be honest with her when she asked him everything she wanted to know? Or would he use misdirection to get his way and her into his bed.

7

Flicking condensation off the tip of his tail, Hamersveld rotated into a flip and went wings vertical. He sliced between two giant redwoods. Thick branches creaking in his blowback, he flew out of the forest. Streetlights played peekaboo, winking behind sloped roofs and chimney stacks. The glow struck his scaled underbelly. His night vision downgraded, shuttering to protect his eyes from the light as he decreased his wing speed and rolled into town on a slow glide.

Glitzy marina up ahead. Boats tied to finger docks, bobbing in the ebb and flow.

Searching the terrain, he scanned the intersecting streets below.

Shop owners locking up. A couple of humans out for a late evening stroll. Nothing beyond the normal ho-hum of a human town.

Normally, he avoided Chelan. Flew around instead of over it, but...not right now. Tonight wasn't about expedience, or avoiding the annoying race mucking up the planet. The deviation in routine was all about Natalie. About giving her a show, along with the time to experience the fullness of a dragon's-eye view.

He hummed in appreciation—for the chance to share what he saw every night when he flew out of the lair. City or rural landscapes. Busy or abandoned places. The subject material didn't matter. Each night brought new views, providing something to see, to pay attention to, and admire while in dragon form.

The south end of Lake Chelan fit the bill.

Pretty and picturesque, the town of Chelan was a tourist trap. All about escaping the city on weekends, specialty shops, and organic food. Tree huggers, and muckety-mucks alike, came from all over the state to boat, fish, mountain bike or golf while soaking up the slower pace away from the city. The vineyards up-lake in Manson didn't hurt either. Humans flocked to the wineries, taking tours in between taste testing. Getting drunk in between cheese courses. Pouring money into small town USA.

Good for the locals.

Better for him, given all the activities happened on the south end of the lake. Few people ventured north into his territory. And no one came near his cabin. The terrain was too rough, and after warning humans away with a dusting of malevolent magic, most stayed out of his area and off what remained of the trails.

Playing in a north wind, he drifted over town, giving his female time to look. A small smile on her face, she shifted to sit cross-legged in his palm. He flexed his talons, opening his paw, providing better sightlines. Sharpened for battle, the blades of his dark blue claws flashed in the moonlight. Natalie barely noticed. She was too busy peering down on small houses and paved streets, the curiosity in her eyes, instead of anger, a balm to his conflicted soul.

"This is cool." Brimming with enthusiasm, she

glanced up at him. "How come no one in town's freaking out?"

"Cloaking spell. No one can see us."

"That's how," she muttered, more to herself than him, answering her own question. The one he knew plagued her—how she'd been taken without anyone outside the athletic center noticing.

He'd picked up on it quick. Every time he saw her in the lair he'd been tempted—oh so tempted—to sit her down and explain. Spill Dragonkind secrets and ease her mind. She hadn't done anything wrong. Wasn't to blame. Couldn't have done anything to change the outcome.

Unlike him, she was guiltless.

Wrong time. Wrong place. Though, he couldn't bring himself to regret it.

If she hadn't been captured, he never would've met her. A circumstance he would've regretted, given how much he enjoyed her company. She settled him in ways he didn't understand and refused to question. Which made him a first-class fool.

Knowing was always better than ignorance. But as he ghosted over town, then circled back around, Hamersveld didn't want the answers. Digging too deep would drag him in dangerous directions. Ones guaranteed to make him yearn to keep her. To turn down the selfish path and risk her life to assuage his own needs.

He clenched his teeth, showing fang.

Silfer's balls, what a joke. *Yearn to keep her.* Mate her. Wrap himself around her and never let go. Like he didn't crave it all, every piece of her, already? Idiot didn't begin to describe him. Especially given what he planned.

"Disappearing act—nifty trick," Natalie grumbled,

dragging his attention back to her. "Guess that's how Dragonkind stays hidden."

"*Um-hmm,*" he murmured, watching her, reading her bioenergy, waiting for her anger to resurface. Goddess knew he deserved it.

He never should've waited.

The instant he spotted her in Cellblock A, he should've broken her out. Said to hell with the breeding program, confronted Ivar with his objections, gathered Natalie up and flown away from 28 Walton Street.

Shoulda.

Coulda.

Woulda.

Regret on top of regret. So much time spent second guessing, but now that he held her, he understood the real cost of inaction—of his uncertainty, of wanting to be accepted by his new pack more than doing the right thing. He wasn't a good male. Never claimed to be, but...in this...he knew Natalie was right. He held all the power. He could've chosen a different path. Found another way—beaten the shit out of Denzeil earlier, kept her safe while he returned Natalie home before she woke inside the lair. Before she realized her freedom had been taken at all.

The fact he hadn't shamed him, dragging guilt to the forefront.

Hristos, he'd fallen from grace. Abandoned his scruples. Ignored primal instinct and forgotten how to be honorable, causing his female to suffer. Which made him an absolute bastard. A male unworthy of claiming Natalie in the way of his kind. The realization raked him like sharp claws. His chest tightened as the pain surfaced. He wanted to turn back the clock.

Longed for a second chance to put her wellbeing first and reclaim his honor.

"Settle down, Hamersveld." Small hand pressed to his palm, Natalie stroked over his scales. Soft touch. Soothing caress. Beautiful compassion. None of which he deserved. "It's over now."

He flinched. *What?*

"I won't let you take me back." Tilting her chin up, she looked at the night sky. She breathed deep and exhaled long. The jagged spike of her aura smoothed, flowing into a gorgeous glow. Drawn to her, unable to control the reflex, he flexed his talons, holding onto her like a greedy child as her expression cleared, and she relaxed. Her gaze flicked up to meet his. "And I can tell you don't want to take me back, either."

Shit. She was reading him. Unearthing his intentions. Cherry picking his thoughts. Using the bond he shared with her to connect the dots, pushing him to face demons long ignored and buried deep.

"You gonna deny it, Hamersveld?"

"Call me Sveld, shaleima," he said, refusing to answer her question. Not wanting to give voice to intention and admit his betrayal of the Razorback's mission out loud.

She opened her mouth to comply.

He flapped his wings and, increasing his speed, rocketed out of town.

Grabbing hold of one of his talons, Natalie laughed.

Mission accomplished. Distraction achieved as she whooped and leaned into the fast flight. Letting go, she shifted in her seat and, spreading her arms wide, pretended she was flying. Energized by her enjoyment, he blasted over the narrows. Trees swayed. Water rippled. Fish scattered beneath the surface as he skimmed the lake. His wingtip slicing through water, he banked into the last turn.

His cabin on the bluff came into view.

Putting on the brakes, he wing-flapped a second and, with a playful flip, dove into the bay. The sheltered lagoon exploded around him. Natalie shrieked, smiling huge as he took her under. Wrapped around her, he laughed as she swirled her arms, turning in the protective circle of his talons, air bubbles rising around her. Relishing the chance to swim, she grinned at him underwater, then kicked upward.

Moonlight shimmered off the surface, showing her the way.

Webbed paws and bladed tail working in the water, he circled below her. He watched a moment, making sure she reached the surface, then shifted into human form. She broke the plane. He registered her gasp. Raking long strands away from her face, she looked around, searching for him.

On a slow rise, he surfaced behind her.

The sky opened up, gifting him with an early spring shower. As raindrops fall, racing over the bay, she tracked him. A strong swimmer, she flicked her hands and pivoted toward him.

Jade green eyes met his.

Pinpricks of pleasure ghosted over his skin.

Treading water, floating with ease, she stared at him. Her bioenergy flared, haloing around her, growing more powerful the longer she studied him. Mining her aura, he tapped into her emotional grid.

Steady.

Sure.

Curious and...completely unafraid.

Her reaction amplified his, making his heart hammer and his soul sing. Unable to look away, he held her gaze and shifted forward. Not a lot. Less than a foot, just enough to telegraph his intention and send water rippling. Natalie didn't flinch or back away. She gave him what he wanted—full eye contact. No shyness or anger. Zero recrimination in her eyes, boatloads of interest.

Fascination ramped need into dangerous territory.

He wanted to go to her. Wanted to touch and taste, spend hours pleasing her.

Hamersveld killed the impulse. Natalie had been held for twenty-seven days—her autonomy stripped away and her right to decide ignored. He needed to give it back. Wanted to return liberty taken and reassure his female. She was in control here. Whatever happened—or didn't—would be driven by her...and her alone.

She drifted closer. "How much time do we have?"

His stomach clenched. Beautiful female. Stunning. So smart she took his breath away. "Tonight. Most of tomorrow."

"Before they come looking for us?"

He nodded.

"Well, then, we'd best make the most of it."

"Natalie, I need you to know—"

"Come here, Sveld." Water swirling around her, she reached out her hand.

Helpless to deny his desperation, he surged into her arms. Waves frothed into white caps as she welcomed him. Burying her hands in his hair, she offered her mouth. Starved for her, he kissed her, groaning as her tongue played against his, becoming drunk on her taste.

"Tonight and tomorrow," she whispered against his mouth.

He murmured her name.

Natalie hummed in return, sending him sideways inside his head.

He'd planned to love her inside his cabin. The first time, anyway, then swim and frolic in the bay afterward. Too bad, not so sad. Best laid intentions, and all that, 'cause...goddamn. Natalie was glorious—the beauty of ocean swells and stormy seas in his arms. Demanding in her desire. So insistent, her fierceness unleashed his own and...

So much for restraint.

Forget gentleness.

He needed her now. Not fifteen minutes from now, but *now*.

Staying away from her had taken its toll. Made him desperate and greedy as he forgot everything and fell over the edge. Meeting his aggression with demands of her own, Natalie ignited in his arms, allowing need to rule, tearing through long-set boundaries to find the heart of him. Emotion broke through the barrier, cracking him wide open as pleasure burned bright and his female showed no mercy, pulling him under, straight into blissful depths of oblivion.

Bad decisions came in threes. Natalie wasn't sure where the law of threes originated, but here, now, as she kissed Hamersveld back, she knew it applied.

Mistake number one—talking to him. Listening to the rumble of his voice seduced her. Deep and smooth, his accent slid beneath the surface of her skin. The hint of sweetness in his growl, the allure of the exotic, tempted her, urging her to drop her guard, take a chance, and get to know him.

Struggling to catch her breath, Natalie smoothed her hands over the tops of his shoulders. Hot skin. Hard muscles. His physic, the sheer size of him, was amazing. Eye-opening. A wonder to behold as he drew her in with soft strokes and savage intensity, making her throb and want and—

Oh, man. What a freaking mess.

Everything about him screwed with her equilibrium.

Now, she didn't know what to do—wade in deeper or splash the hell out. Confusion took another turn inside her head. She couldn't decide. Forget about staying even, or the least bit angry at him. A smart girl would retreat, put her guard up and wield her temper like a weapon—to protect herself and keep him at bay.

A nice thought.

No doubt the way to go, but...

No matter how often she told herself to back away, she held on harder, allowing him to lead her deeper.

Which led her to mistake number two—letting curiosity out of its cage.

A bad decision.

She should've kept the door on all her questions closed. Natalie tried. She really did, but as the crack between her mental jambs widened, inquisitiveness leaked out, causing all kinds of problems. Now, she wanted to know everything about him. Where he was from. How he got mixed up with a kidnapping ring. Why he stayed when he didn't agree with the play and what his cohorts were doing.

Big questions in need of answers.

Which amounted to huge trouble for her.

She'd never been one to let things lie. The need to know how things functioned—the why behind what made gears and people go—fueled her. She liked engines for just that reason. Take it apart. Understand how it worked. Put it back together. Hamersveld was like that, an enigma, a complicated guy in a complex situation...the kind of puzzle she enjoyed solving. Picture unclear. Lots of moving parts. Someone she longed to understand without knowing why.

Compulsion, maybe.

The drive to unlock a mystery, for sure.

Par for her course, but no help to her now.

She was neck deep and sinking fast. Lost in a swift current called desire as he caressed her. His touch light on her skin, callused hands discovering pleasure points, he controlled the flow, possessing her mouth one moment, backing off to nip and tease the next.

And mistake number three?

Well, she was making it. Right now. Responding to Hamersveld. Demanding he give her more. Flying out of smart, landing somewhere south of stupid.

Problem was...hard as she tried, she couldn't bring herself to care. The taste of him tripped her up, tipped her scales, driving her toward him instead of away. Man, oh man. He felt unbelievably good. So beautiful in her arms. So strong and hard against her, she tightened her grip, running her hands through his hair, playing in the shoulder-length strands, wanting to fall heart-first into trust and...*believe*.

Believe in the promise of him.

Believe that, somehow, no matter how crazy, things would work out in the end.

His tongue stroked along hers.

Natalie lost what remained of her mind. She went all in, refusing to pull back and push away. A glimmer of self-preservation shifted through the back of her brain. Like a weed riding in a rushing river, Natalie allowed it to stream by without catching hold.

Foolish, maybe, but confinement had taught her something important. Tomorrow always arrived too late. Here and now was all she owned, the only time promised. How he made her feel—honored, protected, valued—mattered more than any regrets she might have in the morning.

She wanted him.

He was desperate for her.

Natalie sensed his need. Waves of desire crashed over him and through her as water swirled, and they slow danced in the middle of the bay. Kissing. Touching. Him learning every inch of her. Her reacting to him. Each caress an exploration. Every tease and taste a revelation. No one had ever wanted her this way, spent so much time, cared enough to bathe her in bliss. Which left only one way for her go—toward him, instead of away.

Wise or not, she would have him. Take everything he offered and pray it didn't go bad when it came time for her to leave.

Deep in the erotic fog he ensnared her in, she drew her fingertips along his jaw. Day old stubble prickled her skin, enlivening her senses as she licked over his bottom lip. She retreated a little. He growled, trying to bring her back.

Natalie smiled against his mouth. "What does *shaleima* mean?"

"Water lily in Dragonese," he murmured, raking his teeth along her throat. Her belly curled, making her tighten deep inside. Lord, he was good at that— arresting gentleness with just the right amount bite. She shuddered as he sucked on her pulse point, then breathed deep, scenting her like a wolf did his mate. "You smell like lilies of the valley—fresh and pure...beautiful."

"Sveld," she whispered, overwhelmed by him, needing more than a slow dance beneath the stars. "I need your skin against mine. Your scent all over me."

He growled against her throat and returned to her mouth. Kissing her deep, he shoved his hands under her clothes. Big hands moving fast, he stripped her out of her pants. Cupping her bottom, he traced the edge of her underwear. Lace got dragged down her legs. As she kicked free, he yanked the sweater and sports bra over her head, freeing her and—

Ecstasy. Skin-to-skin, all of him against her.

Pleasure sparked, cascading everywhere he touched her.

Breathing hard, lost in the beauty of him, she whispered his name.

"Goddess, you're soft. So soft, Natalie."

She moaned in appreciation as his hands drifted over her. His fingertips ghosted over her hip and in, dipping between her thighs. Relief flowed into delight. Clever fingers. Gentle strokes. Bliss brought to life. She arched in his arms as he ventured deeper, pushing her higher, holding her on the edge, refusing to let her fall.

Desperation took hold.

Hitching her knee over his hip, she undulated against him, trying to push the pace. He refused to allow it, controlling the surge and release, making her follow his lead. Water danced around them. As the warm rush splashed against her skin, Natalie raked her nails over his back. Hard muscles flexed. She gasped, bucking as he found a sensitive spot inside her.

"Sveld...Sveld...I need—"

"I know what you need," he growled, increasing the rhythm, working her harder.

"Now."

"Not yet."

"Handsome," she rasped, heart thumping, body humming, imploring him. "It's been so long. I can't wait."

"You're going to have to, *shaleima*. I like to watch. And you're going to show me."

Big hand cupping her bottom, he rolled her into each advance and retreat. Gaze riveted to her face, he forced her to the brink, then pulled her back. Over and over. Again and again. Slick heat made the ride easy. His pace nearly killed her. She was primed, on the edge, so ready to ride for real, she begged for the pleasure. He murmured to her, talking dirty, driving her closer, refusing to let her fall.

"Gorgeous, Natalie. Give me more," he said against her cheek. "Ride, *shaleima*. I wanna watch you come... feel you around my fingers...before I take you."

Pleasure-pain coiled in her belly. "I...oh, God."

"Take what you want, Natalie. Get yourself there."

Hips rolling, so aroused she hurt, Natalie shook her head. "I can't. I—"

Pressing two fingers inside her, he pressed his thumb against her clit. Firm pressure, a fast swirl drove her higher up the peak. He flexed his hand, changing the angle. Ecstasy hit hard, shiny and bright, obliterating her senses. Natalie ignited, burning for him as she threw her head back and pulsed around him.

Her cry raced over the water, then ricocheted, echoing across the lake.

With a hum of enjoyment, Hamersveld dipped his head. Hot breath ghosted over her breast as he licked her nipple. Fingers curled inside her, he nipped the sensitive bud, sending pleasure soaring. She gasped. He growled and, bathing her in delight, sucked hard, pushing her over the edge again. Exploding off the top she flew into oblivion on the wings he provided, shuddering, body rocking, moaning his name.

Another gentle swirl of his fingers.

Another soul-stealing suck against her breast.

Overwhelmed, Natalie clung to him, feeling the rush of another orgasm on the way. His mouth jumped to her throat. She bucked as the sharp edge of his teeth grazed her. Long, strong fingers stroking deep, he shoved her toward an even sharper edge.

Gasping, she abandoned all pride. "Please, please, *please*."

"Say my name while you beg."

"Sveld, please," she moaned, pulsing around his fingers.

His hand left her. A slight shift. A rough nudge. A merciless thrust and—

She received all of him.

"Yesss."

"Fucking hell," he said through clenched teeth, buried to the hilt inside her. Her inner muscles rippled around him. He groaned as she settled, perfecting their fit. "So hot and slick. My Natalie. My beautiful female. You feel amazing."

The compliment should've pleased her.

Natalie was too far gone. She needed him to move, to take her back to the place where nothing and no one but him mattered. "Move, handsome. Please, you gotta—"

Snarling at her, Hamersveld retreated and returned. Each stroke hot, hard and heavy. Water rolled into waves. She moved with him, tilting her hips, welcoming his possession. He showed no mercy, loving her hard, spinning her out of her mind into her soul. As the seam split, emotion rushed through the gap, and she whispered to him, telling how beautiful he was, how much she wanted him, admitting her need, giving him every little piece of her.

Dangerous.

Unadvisable.

Mistake number four—the stealer of souls.

But as he made love to her, murmuring words of his own, she let go of illusion. For better or worse, in this moment, Hamersveld had become her everything.

Her home and safe haven, the only place on earth she wanted to be and knew she would always belong.

Water swirling, relishing the give and take, Natalie soared on the wings of delight. Her body throbbed. Her mind went blank. She sank into boneless drift, listening as rapture tore Hamersveld apart, threw him over the edge and he fell, gifting her every little piece of himself in return.

9

Body heavy, brain scrambled, Hamersveld stirred. Warm. Content. More sated than he'd ever been in his life, he drifted in mental fog. Awareness seeped in a little at a time. The ebb and flow murmured to him. Thoughts solidified and began towing him toward the surface. His muscles twitched as chilly air nipped at his bare skin. He blinked and—

Water washed over his feet.

Struggling to get his bearings, he moved, shifting slightly...and realized two things at once. The first—he wasn't in the bay anymore. And second—he was lying on the beach, still buried to the hilt inside Natalie, nestled between the spread of her thighs.

Worried he was too heavy for her, he planted a forearm in the sand and adjusted their fit. Pleasure curled through him, tightening the base of his spine. With a low groan, he pressed deeper, opened his eyes and... saw a wealth of red hair.

His lips curved in appreciation as satisfaction whispered through him. Goddess blessed him. His female, so crazy beautiful.

Flexing his hand, he sifted through the bright, sunset strands. Thick, unbelievably soft, her tresses clung, wrapping around and in between his fingers as he lifted his head from the cove of her throat. The movement made his vision blur. He blinked it away, trying to figure out where he'd landed. He didn't remember much. Blistering pleasure had overwhelmed him. Sent him sideways inside his head, but that was no excuse.

A warrior never dropped his guard, but as he stared at the narrow stretch of beach beneath the bluff and his cabin, Hamersveld refused to berate himself. His dragon half had done its job, picked up the slack, watching his back, keeping Natalie safe, permitting him to lose control while he concentrated on her.

A real surprise.

He never lost his head—or sight of his surroundings. Given the brutality of his enemies, doing either was dangerous.

Clearly, Natalie had loved him into oblivion. Vanquished his dragon half. Launched him into orbit. Dragged him so deep into ecstasy, he abandoned the usual caution and good sense. A first for him. He enjoyed bedding females—no question—but what his redhead gave him wasn't that. Nothing about her approached shallow. She went deeper. Was *more*. More exquisite. More intense. More...*everything*.

"Silfer's balls," he muttered, bowing his head.

Raking wet hair out of his face, Hamersveld took more of his weight from her and leaned back to look at her. Eyes closed, breathing deep and even, Natalie lay relaxed beneath him. Bathed in the heat of her aura, he studied the glow, then turned his attention and mined her bioenergy, checking her vitals.

Happy. Relaxed. Satisfied and sleepy, but not asleep.

His gaze roamed her face. Auburn eyelashes and

arched brows. Heart-shaped face and high, sloping cheekbones. Beauty made real, the power of the Meridian brought to life.

Fucking hell.

He was in real trouble. Down the rabbit hole with a female his dragon half wanted so desperately, the beast's reaction sped past yearning, right into obsession. The spike in his already dangerous fixation didn't bode well—for Natalie or him. His need for her threw a crook into his plans, making him question everything. Was freeing her the right thing to do? Now that he knew the beauty of her—her taste, how she fit against him, and he felt inside her—could he really let her go? Doing the right thing always came at a cost, but...hell. One night and day with her wasn't going to be enough.

He needed a lifetime. Wanted forever, but...

No way that would happen.

He refused to risk her. Which would happen if he came clean with his pack.

The instant his secret surfaced and Ivar realized he couldn't sire children, Natalie would be taken from him and given to another. A male capable of siring sons—or the daughters his friend tried to engineer through his science experiments—would be assigned to her. Ivar might respect and love him, but he would give no quarter. Not in this. Natalie and the others had been taken for one reason—to unlock the curse and correct a mistake.

Ivar was working an end-around, trying to out-science the Goddess of All Things and wipe out the deity's cruel decree. The one that left his kind unable to sire girl infants of their own. A vulnerable state, unacceptable to most as it made Dragonkind males reliant on human females. Not fair by any stretch, but...it was what it *was*. A punishment laid on his race, driven by a pissed off Goddess and powerful magic. A circumstance not subject to change.

Or so he thought, until he met Ivar.

Whether his friend's experiment would work was anyone's guess.

Natalie and the other females comprised the first group. Each had been prepped with a serum Ivar believed would allow Dragonkind to sire both genders. So...no chance of changing his friend's mind. Ivar never pulled his punches. If Hamersveld shared the truth of his infertility, he'd lose his female.

Full stop.

No passing *GO* or collecting two hundred dollars.

The game would be over before it began.

Clenching his teeth, Hamersveld shook his head. His decision was sound. No matter how much he wanted to, he couldn't keep her. Mating her wouldn't solve the problem of the breeding program. Or loosen Ivar's obsession with siring a daughter of his own.

Heart heavy, chest so tight it hurt, he dipped his head and kissed his female. Softly. Sweetly. Rousing her with gentle caresses. "*Shaleima*."

With a hum, Natalie shifted beneath him. "I can still feel you."

"I'm still inside you.'

Raising her knees, she wrapped her legs around his waist. "Nice."

Loving the feel of her hands in his hair, he licked into her mouth. She kissed him back, dueling with his tongue, delivering her taste, giving as good as he gave.

Ready for another round, he hardened inside her.

"Hmm, yeah." Tilting her head back, she broke the kiss and rocked into him. "Let's go again."

Hamersveld didn't argue.

He moved instead.

Gripping her hips, he kept their connection tight and rolled onto his back. Wet sand shifted beneath him. Waves washed onto shore, washing over his feet. Bliss whispered his name as Natalie settled on top.

Playing with her hair, he pulled the thick strands away from her face. "You're turn to do the work, Natalie. Ride me, *shaleima*. Give me a show."

Green eyes lit with mischief, she planted her hand on his chest and pushed upright. Her heat gripped him harder. He sucked in a breath. She smiled and, holding his gaze, undulated on him. Pink tipped breasts quivered as she arched her spine, rolled her hips, gifting him with her beauty...and an erotic dance the likes of which he'd never forget.

Gaze glued to her, he felt and watched her move. Every slick slide. Each soul-stealing retreat. Pleasure and pain engulfed him. Pleasure for her generous nature and beautiful spirit. Pain for the fact she'd soon be gone, leaving him alone, bereft without her.

But he had her now.

And so, he timed his thrusts, moving with her, caressing her skin, learning what made her moan as she rode. And he watched, body tightening, desire rising, his need for her blowing past his defenses. He growled as she bore down and—

Holy hell. He wasn't going to make it. Was going to come before she did if she kept up the tease and taunt.

Holding on by a thread, he surged beneath her.

Long hair brushing her breasts, she met and held his gaze. "You crying mercy?"

"Fuck." Cupping her bottom, he slid his other hand across her belly, aiming for the spot that drove her wild.

She knocked his hand away. "Ask for mercy, handsome."

"Natalie," he rasped, bucking inside her, clinging to control.

"Ask."

Enthralled by her game, he shook his head.

She upped the pace.

Heart hammering, bliss burned through him. "*Shaleima*. Beautiful, I'm gonna—"

"Do it, Sveld. Ask me."

He hesitated, loving her fierceness, until he couldn't hold back anymore. "Mercy, Natalie...mercy."

Given her due, his female bared her teeth. Expression almost feral, she slid her hand down to her curls. Her fingers swirled, stroking his shaft as she circled her clit. His mind blurred. Pleasure tightened its grip. Rocking against him, she clenched hard as she came, snarling his name. He jacked upright and, ass planted in the sand, wrapped his arms around her. Her wet heat milked him. He groaned and let go, coming with her, holding her down, filling her full.

"God, yeah," she said, gasping against the top of his head. "So good."

Breathing hard, unable to answer, he hugged her close, fighting to recover. Her energy nipped him. Unable to resist, he set his mouth against her throat and connected to the Meridian. Nourishing energy burned through her into him. He drank deep. Natalie mewed and, hands in his hair, lifted her chin, offering herself, accepting his need, feeding him from the source.

His dragon half rose to greet its female.

A different kind of delight streamed through him.

Cosmic threads tied him up, strapped him down and sank deep, burning her imprint onto his soul as he praised her, acknowledging her gift, amazed by her all over again. Wrapped around him, Natalie sighed and settled in, hiding nothing, giving everything, patient in the face of his hunger.

A while later, she shivered, and Hamersveld resurfaced, so content it took him a minute to realize he'd lost himself in her again. *Hristos*, she was something. So fierce as she loved him, she made him made forget everything but her. Drawing in a breath, he opened his eyes and, retreating a little, looked at her.

"Hey." Sleepy voice. Unfocused gaze. Aura burning bright...still under the effects of an intense energy feeding. "You okay?"

"Hard to tell." Fighting a smile, he ran his hands over her. Soft skin against his. Gorgeous spirit on display. Worried about him when it should be the other way around. He'd taken his fill. Drank deep. Was so full magic frothed in his veins, threatening to spill over. Shocking. A little alarming. Something, he'd never once experienced...in three hundred years of living. "You fucked me into oblivion...again."

Eyes sparkling, she smiled, then unable to hold it back, yawned.

"Tired?"

"A little, but mostly relaxed."

"Good," he said, relieved he hadn't taken too much. "Ready to eat? Or do you want to swim before breakfast."

"Swim. Or maybe just float awhile."

His mouth curved.

His kind of female—beauty, brains, and an unapologetic water nymph. No one else matched her. Everything about Natalie called to him. Which made him remember all the reasons he mustn't get too attached to the female in his arms.

Regret clawed through him.

Hamersveld banished the pang, pushing it aside as he called on his magic. Water rose in the center of the inlet, rolling into a ten-foot wave. The surge rumbled toward shore. Still straddling him, Natalie popped onto her knees and glanced over her shoulder. Her breath caught as the wet curl hit, tumbling around them. Warm water picked them up. She shrieked, clinging to him as the lake dragged them off the beach toward the middle of the bay.

Body surfing beside him, Natalie laughed.

Hamersveld grinned as he watched her, controlling the flow, enjoying her enthusiasm, giving her a ride even as his heart grew heavy, and he wondered how, when the time came, he'd manage to let her go.

10

Arms stretched above her head, Natalie lay belly-down in the middle of the king-sized bed. Soft sheets tangled around her. Comfortable mattress beneath her. A pillow stuffed beneath her hips, tilting her bottom up as Hamersveld kissed his way up her spine.

His teeth grazed the nape of her neck.

She twitched in reaction.

"Don't move." The low growl raised goose bumps on her skin. She shivered. He pressed deep. Her knees slid across cotton as he spread her legs wider, thrusting hard to her center. "Hold still, Natalie and take me."

Wrists tied with silk rope to the headboard, she didn't have much choice. He'd taken it all away, introducing her to bondage, overloading her senses, making her submit as he took her from behind. Each hard, slick stroke rocked her. The brush of his skin, the strength of his body, drove her higher. She moaned, the pleasure so intense she fisted her hands in the sheets, trying to do as he commanded, but...

God. She couldn't catch her breath.

Her body burned. Her mind spiraled, making it

impossible to decide—obey and receive the orgasm he promised, or misbehave and get what he threatened... her very first spanking.

Oh, the temptation.

She'd never played this way before, but as he continued to tease her, she knew what he wanted—payback. He wanted her to beg for mercy. Was angling to hear the words she made him say on the beach. Big hands caressing her, he advanced and retreated, driving her mad, making her world tilt.

"Sveld," she gasped as he pushed deeper, bottoming out inside her.

"Don't bother, *shaleima*. Begging won't save you."

"What will?"

"My benevolence."

She moaned. "You don't have any."

"A pity for you. Nothing left to do now but surrender."

Surrender.

The word should've pissed her off. Made her wary. Prompted her to fight.

She gave in instead, so in love with the way Hamersveld loved her, she let it all go. Became his in the moment, just as she'd been all day. Natalie hadn't fought the fall. She'd taken the plunge without compunction. Hamersveld made it easy—talking between bouts of lovemaking, feeding her, holding her while she slept, asking questions about her life, listening when she told him about her parents, the dyslexia, and dropping out of college.

No judgment in his eyes, just warm acceptance. A rare gift. One of true belonging, of finding a place in the world where she fit.

Nipping the back of her shoulder, Hamersveld bit down and held on, marking her with his teeth. Rapture rumbled through her as he licked over the small bite, bathing her in heat, making her squirm. Unable to stop the impulse, she rolled her hips, pressing back against him.

"You moved."

Muscles clenched deep inside her. "I—"

His big hand met her backside. The sharp slap rolled into a beautiful sting. Pleasure detonated, and she flew, throbbing around him.

"Fuck," he murmured, spanking her again.

As she pulsed, he jerked her onto her knees. Strokes long and hard, he wrapped his hand in her hair and, controlling her completely, drove her into another mind-blistering orgasm. Burning for him, she accepted it all, loving the sound and feel of him, using her body to pleasure his, enthralled by his intensity as he gave her everything.

He groaned and fell forward, covering her with his heat.

Cheek pressed to the sheets, she relaxed beneath him, reveling in the aftershocks, letting him warm her.

Nuzzling her temple, he sighed, the sound full of contentment. "You're going to kill me."

She smiled. "You're the one who tied me up."

"Couldn't help myself," he murmured. "You look beautiful in my ropes, Natalie. Had to see it for myself, just once before..."

He paused, and she understood.

Hamersveld didn't want to say it, but with daylight waning, it was almost time.

Time for her to put how she felt aside. Time to be brave, leave the bed, and him behind. Time for them to say goodbye.

The idea spun her full circle. Her mind and heart rebelled. Beyond stupid. She knew what was coming. Hamersveld hadn't shied from the truth. When she asked, he explained, giving it to her straight, laying out her future in clear terms if she stayed with him. He hadn't liked scaring her. She saw the displeasure—his concern for her—in his eyes when he told her about the breeding program, but at least now, she understood what Ivar and the Razorback pack intended and where she stood in relation to it.

So unfair. All avenues, but one, were closed her.

She needed to leave before the sun went down and Razorbacks left the lair for the night. Which meant leaving Kasi behind without doing what she promised—calling the authorities and rescuing the others. Natalie wanted to, but lacked what every good rescue plan required—a hard target. She didn't have the necessary information. No address to share. No neighborhood to point the police toward. No evidence either. Just what she knew to be true, and no one would believe.

Her heart squeezed, sending pain spiraling through her.

"I don't wanna go," she whispered, giving voice to despair, to a truth she'd been grappling with all day.

"I know, but you have to, *shaleima*. I can't protect you from what's coming." Mouth brushing the back of her shoulder, he reached up. A quick tug, and the knot came free. With gentle hands, Hamersveld untied her, rubbing her wrists, tracing the faint marks. Flipping her over, he kissed her softly, then tucked her close, not wanting to let her go any more than she wanted him to. "I've prepared everything. New identification papers for you. A vehicle, money...you'll lack for nothing."

"Except you."

"Except me," he said, the regret in his tone so thick her heart hurt.

Her throat tightened. Breathing through the pain, she hung onto her tears. "What if I'm pregnant, Sveld? We didn't use protec—"

"You aren't, baby."

"How can you be sure?"

"Magic."

"Right."

Magic. The currency of Dragonkind. Unique to his species. Unmatched by the human race or anything else on the planet. He'd given her those lessons too.

"Sun's going to set soon, Natalie."

"Time to go."

"Yeah," he murmured into the top of her head. Giving her a squeeze, he dragged her to the edge of the bed. "Get dressed. I'll get the bag."

Forcing her muscles to unlock, she let him go. The action felt unnatural. As though she was making the biggest mistake of her life. But as she watched him conjure a pair of jeans and cross the one room cabin—the tattoo bracketing his spine rippling over his gorgeous muscles—she did as he asked and reached for the clothes folded neatly on the bedside table. With quick hands and a heavy heart, she dressed in silence and laced up her running shoes.

Stepping away from the bed, she moved toward the kitchen island and the black duffle on the countertop. Her future sat in that bag. Everything she needed to make a clean break and a new life.

Closing the fridge door, Hamersveld turned toward her. He held up a soft cooler, then set it down beside the duffle. "Food for the road. Nothing fancy. A couple of sandwiches, fresh fruit, power bars, bottles of water."

Not trusting her voice, Natalie nodded.

"Come here, baby."

Skirting the countertop, she met him on the other side of the island.

He unzipped the bag and pulled out a travel pouch. "Info for your account in the Caymans and all the paperwork for your new ID—passport, birth certificate and social insurance number—are in the pouch. Driver's license and credit cards are in the wallet. A change of clothes and travelling money, fifty-grand in cash, is in the bag."

Her breath caught. "This took time to prepare."

"Twenty-seven days, eleven hours, and forty-three minutes."

"Sveld, you—"

"I won't lie, Natalie." His brow furrowed. "I fought it, but I knew the moment I saw you, I wasn't going to leave you in Cellblock A. Or allow you to be used to further Ivar's cause."

Tucking the pouch back inside the bag, he yanked on the zipper, closing the bag with a vicious tug. She knew what his actions meant. He was struggling to stay in control and hide his upset by issuing orders. And she needed to let him. The urge to give him that gift—soothe him anyway she could—was simply too strong to ignore.

Steeling herself, she locked down her emotions and reached for the wallet. He handed it to her. Butter soft leather sliding against her fingertips, she popped the clasp. Protected by a plastic face, she ran her finger over the license and her new name. "Natalie Kristiansen."

"My mother's surname."

Another piece of him. A gift beyond what he'd already given her. "It's beautiful."

His throat worked as he reached into the front pocket of his jeans. Drawing a breath, he set a fancy key fob in her hand. "For the truck parked out back. A Hybrid. Tank's full, so you won't have to stop for a while."

Unable to hold on any longer, tears slid over her bottom lashes.

"*Shaleima*. Beautiful, don't cry. Please, don't cry."

"Sorry," she said, voice hitching. "I just—"

"I know. Me too." Reaching out, he reeled her in, wrapping his arms around her. Holding on hard, she absorbed his warmth, memorized his voice and the way he felt against her. Hugging her close, he pressed his mouth to the top of her head. "Remember everything I told you. Make a fresh start. Nothing and no one familiar. If you return to your old life, Ivar will find you."

"I'll remember."

"I'm sorry, Natalie, but this is the way it has to be. It's the only way I can keep you safe."

More tears threatened. "Thank you for everything."

"Take care of yourself," he murmured, kissing her temple. "Settle near the water, on the ocean. I'll imagine you there—happy, strong, in a beautiful place that matches your spirit."

"At least five hundred miles, right? As long as I stay that far away, you can't track me."

"Exactly right. You come any closer, break through that barrier, I'll sense you. I won't be able to let you go a second time." Pulling away, he cupped her face. Expression serious, he met her gaze, the resignation in his eyes difficult to take. His mouth brushed hers. Once. Twice. A third time, before he dropped his hands and stepped away. "Go, Natalie, before I'm unable to let you."

A dark chasm opened inside her.

Hollowness took hold.

Natalie wanted to scream at the unfairness. She obeyed instead and, shattered by pain, grabbed the bags off the countertop. Each step leaden, she crossed to the door and, without a backward glance, left the man she wanted, but couldn't have, standing in the kitchen with her heart in his hands.

11

As the door clicked closed behind Natalie, Hamersveld nearly lost his mind. He locked his frame, muscles tight and mind screaming, rooting himself to floor. Pain spiraled through him. Goddess. He couldn't breathe.

He couldn't breathe.

Dragon half rebelling, the beast sharpened his senses, torturing him with sounds. Heart hammering, chest hurting, he listened to her footfalls rap across the bluff. Agony carved a bloody trail through his mind. Fighting for each breath, he focused on the pain, forcing air into his lungs, then back out again. Grief welled from mental wounds and spilled over, the sorrow so profound he swayed on his feet as the truck door opened and closed.

The engine started.

He heard the motor shift into gear.

All terrain tires rolled over stone, heading toward the trail.

Torment erupted from his throat, giving voice to his anguish.

Fighting to stay upright, Hamersveld flexed his

fists as she drove down the narrow path that lead to the main road on the north end of Lake Chelan. The one he'd cleared through thick brush and tall pines for her. Weeks ago. Before he understood what he would do—how it would feel, the heartbreak of letting Natalie go.

He'd known doing right by her would cost him.

He just hadn't counted on it ripping him apart.

And as he stood in his cabin, a place meant to be a sanctuary, all he felt was gutted. Wrecked by the knowledge he would never see her again. Never get to hold her. Never see her smile. Never be the male she made him imagine himself capable of being. Honorable, for once. Worthy of her attention. Her *everything* in the same way she'd become his.

Such a short amount of time.

One night. One unbelievable day. That's all he'd ever get.

Bowing his head, Hamersveld raked his hands through his hair. He tugged on the strands, welcoming the discomfort, needing to feel something other than devastating loss. Everything hurt. Muscles and bones. Mind and heart. Even the black, bottomless pit he called a soul. But even as the feeling swamped him, he acknowledged an undeniable truth. In making her go, he'd saved her life. Given her a future. One without him, but his female deserved a long life full of happiness, not one cut short by bringing a Dragonkind infant into the world.

He suffered no illusions.

The world he inhabited was a harsh one. Unkind to human females. Devastating to the males who loved them. Oh, rumors about energy-fuse and mating marks abounded—the magical bond necessary to ensure a female survived birthing a Dragonkind babe. Hamersveld didn't believe any of it. He was three hundred years old. In all that time, he'd never seen a mating mark, never mind met a male who'd experienced the glory of energy-fuse.

Energy-fuse.

He scoffed. Nothing but misdirection. Wishful thinking, little more than hopes and dreams. All of it touted by males desperate for connection and a family of their own.

Too bad he couldn't deny the allure. Or fight the yearning. Not anymore. The hours spent with Natalie had changed him in ways he struggled to identify and didn't understand. Which spun him in unfamiliar directions. Into dangerous places. Ones a warrior of his caliber couldn't afford to go, never mind stay.

Raking his hands over his face, Hamersveld stared at his bare feet. He needed to get his shit together and his head screwed on straight. The sooner, the better. The instant night fell, Ivar would track him. The bond he shared with the male was a strong one. His friend would have no trouble finding his cabin on Lake Chelan. A simple ping, and he'd lock on, take flight from 28 Walton Street with one object in mind—to hammer him and recoup the HE female Ivar believed belonged to the breeding program.

Hamersveld bared his teeth.

Not going to happen.

Natalie was well on her way. Driving away from Dragonkind, instead of caught in its snarled web. She was safe now. Secure inside her new future. Far away from Ivar's scientific experiments and the warriors he commanded. None of the other Razorbacks could track her. He'd made sure of it, keeping every male who expressed interest away from her. He was the only one who could find her. Ivar would try and force the issue—insist Hamersveld track and retrieve her—but what his friend didn't know would come back to bite him.

Hamersveld hated to use what he knew against his friend. He liked the idea of threatening Ivar about as much as ripping his own tail off. But he wouldn't hesitate to protect Natalie. His female needed to stay free and clear. He'd put his future—his life—on the line for her. No one would get in the way of her safety and his sacrifice. Ivar included.

With a sigh, he dropped his hands and looked around. His gaze landed on the bed. Messy sheets. Dented pillows. Silk ropes tied to the headboard. Thick duvet in a pile on the floor. He needed to clean up the mess, then jump in the shower, and scrub all trace of her away—off his skin, out of his cabin and his mind, but...

Hamersveld turned toward the liquor cabinet instead.

Flipping the door open, he grabbed a bottle of Jim Beam by the throat. He stared at the label a moment. Black, Extra Aged...Ivar's favorite. Why he had it in his cupboard, Hamersveld didn't know. He rarely drank, but when he did, the tab he rang up included Heineken and little else.

Frowning at the bourbon, he cracked it open with a vicious twist. The seal broke. The smell of alcohol rolled into the air. He breathed deep, then took the plunge, drinking straight from the bottle. As he swallowed, Hamersveld realized he couldn't do it. He wasn't ready to wash Natalie away yet. He was too raw, needed the scent of her all over him to soothe his dragon half and regain a sense of equilibrium. And speaking of which...

"Fen," he said, the urge to see his wren overpowering. "Up and at 'em, buddy."

A beautiful burn shimmered over his back as Fen woke and obeyed. Movement flickered behind him as his wren unplugged from the tattoo along his spine and materialized behind him.

A horned head nudged his shoulder.

Shooting more J.B., he rubbed his hand over Fen's snout. Smooth scales slid against his palm as his wren leaned into the caress. He scratched behind his small horns. Fen purred. The familiar sound soothed him, unlocking his chest, allowing him to breathe around the pain.

Turning away from the counter, he skirted the island and, shoving stools aside, sat down, back to the cabinets, legs outstretched, bottle in hand. Attuned to his mood, Fen curled up on the pine-plank floor and, setting his head in his lap, settled in beside him.

Hamersveld welcomed the affection. He needed steady. Craved a return to normal. Yearned to forget, and so he lifted the bottle and drank deep. Bourbon burned down his throat and hit his belly. Warmth spread, dulling the pain, blunting his edges as he stared at the windows. Darkened by magic, protecting him from deadly UV rays, the triple-panes lightened little by little, reacting as the sun set and night overcame day.

He took another drink.

It wouldn't be long now. Ivar was no doubt pacing inside 28 Walton Street, eager to be set free by night, fly north and kick his ass.

Working on the J.B., Hamersveld stroked Fen's head and waited. Time spun away as his mind drifted and he relived the beauty of his female. Resting the back of his head against the island, he closed his eyes and committed her to memory—hearing her laughter, seeing her green eyes flash with amusement or ire, recalling the fierce way she loved him. So much spirit in such a small package. Still, she'd packed a punch, undoing him moment by moment, ruining him one soft sigh and gentle caress at a time.

He blew out a long breath.

Drink. Remember. Repeat.

Nothing else to do, but mourn and curse and—

A thump drifted into the cabin from outside. The deck creaked. A soft growl swirled through the air. Hamersveld opened his eyes and looked through the now clear windows. Raising the bottle, he took another drink as Ivar uncloaked. Blood-red scales gleaming in moonlight, smoke rising from his nostrils, flame flicking down his spiked spine, his friend's horned head swung as he looked around.

Pale pink eyes aglow, Ivar bared his fangs.

Fen sprang to attention. As he rose to sit upright beside him, the rows of dagger-like needles encircling his neck flipped out, standing on end. His wren hissed. Hamersveld murmured, reassuring Fen as Ivar shifted into human form. Expression set to pissed off, his friend stomped his feet into his combat boots and, with a flick of his fingers, gestured to the sky, waving his personal guard away.

Hamersveld blinked.

Well, hell. He hadn't expected that—for Ivar to call off Rampart and the others. The move signaled something. Gave him hope. Ivar might be angry, but he wasn't out of control. And as he watched his friend cross the deck toward his cabin, he marveled at the change in the commander of the Razorback pack.

Ivar planned to talk first and pass judgment second. No extra muscle needed. No witnesses required for the showdown. An unexpected gesture. A kindness granted as Ivar prepared to give him the benefit of the doubt, time to explain before trying to tear him apart.

Eyes on the male approaching like a thundercloud, Hamersveld tipped the bottle again.

Unleashing a wave of magic, Ivar hammered the French doors. The pair flew open. Heavy duty hinges squawked, then whiplashed, swinging the panels back toward the wall. With a murmur, Hamersveld lessened the impact, slowing the backlash, keeping the glass from shattering as Ivar crossed the threshold.

Heavy footfalls thudded across wooden floor.

Ivar raged past the couch, pink gaze searching. The second he saw him, his friend stopped short. He ran a critical eye over him. "Jesus, Sveld. What happened to you?"

"She ruined me," he said...and why not? Honesty might not always be the best policy, but right now, he couldn't bring himself to be anything else. "I'm completely fucking wrecked."

Confusion winged across Ivar's face. His gaze left him to search the inside of the cabin, then snapped back. "Where is she?"

"Gone."

Ivar's brows collided. "You let her go?"

Prepared for Ivar's explosive temper, he braced. "Yeah, and don't bother asking. I won't track her. Natalie's safe, and going to stay that way."

A muscle flexing in his jaw, Ivar glared at him. "Then you own me a high energy female to replace her."

Perfect. Just what he wanted his friend to say. The game was afoot, and he was about to be crowned the victor. "How about the female across the street? The one you've been visiting in the little A-frame."

Ivar sucked in a breath. His mouth opened. No sound came out. He closed it again.

"Didn't think I knew about her, did you?"

"Shit," Ivar said, sounding shell-shocked. "How? I've been careful. I've been—"

"Not careful enough." Raising the bottle, Hamersveld took another swig. "Who do you think's been covering your ass every time you sneak out of the lair to visit her?"

Hands planted on his hips, Ivar bowed his head. A second later, he put his boots in gear, skirted the armchair and, avoiding Fen, sat down on the other side of him. Shoulders slumped against the cabinetry, he gestured to the J.B. "Give me that."

Hamersveld passed him the bottle.

His friend took a drink. "Anyone else know?"

"Don't think so, but..." He shrugged. "Rampart's smart. Very observant. Wouldn't be surprised if—"

"I'm fucked."

"Welcome to the club, brother."

Ivar huffed, took another pull, then handed him the bourbon.

He accepted it, downed more, then gave it back. Quiet settled as they sat shoulder-to-shoulder, both lost in thought, sharing the bottle. As bourbon disappeared, Hamersveld stroked his hand over Fen and stared out at the lake. Water sparkled beneath a clear sky and moonlight, taunting him with the midnight swim he'd shared with Natalie.

"You know," Tipping his head back, Ivar stared at the ceiling. One moment turned into ten. His friend downed another swallow, glancing at him from the corner of his eye. "I was afraid this would happen."

"What?"

"You and the female. I watched you watching her. Your fixation with her, Sveld...fuck, brother...playing with fire."

"Yeah." Accepting the J.B. from his friend, Hamersveld picked at the paper label stuck to the bottle. "I couldn't stand it, Ivar. Seeing her in that cell, knowing she was suffering. No way I could turn away. She's...hell, I don't know...everything."

"I feel your pain."

Hamersveld raised a brow. "The female across the street?"

"Sasha Cooper. Beautiful, smart, a remarkable female," Ivar said, resignation in his tone. "Total pain in my ass. I don't understand it. Been fighting my attraction to her, the blinding need, but I just can't—"

"Win?"

"Leave her alone," Ivar said at the same time.

Hamersveld snorted. "Sounds like I resisted the pull longer than you."

Ivar laughed, no humor, all despair. "Probably."

"What are you going to do?"

"About Sasha?"

"The Meridian realigns in three weeks, Ivar." He raised a brow. "You really going to risk her?"

"Fuck, man...she's not even prepped with the serum. I couldn't bring myself to do it. Can't bear to lock her down in Cellblock A. Can't stay away from her, so..." Clenching his teeth, he shook his head. "*Da,* I'm fucked."

"Not necessarily. There's always lockdown."

"No place to go. I didn't build a vault inside the new lair. Didn't think I'd need one, so I never prepared the contingency."

"28 Walton might not have one, but I know a place

that does," Hamersveld said, mind churning, formatting a plan on the fly.

"Where?"

"The Cascades. Inside the old army base."

"Where you've been holding the competition?"

"It's beat to shit, but also equipped with a nuclear fallout shelter. Two hundred feet underground. The walls are thick, five feet of concrete and steel. With a few modifications, it'll lock down tight. No way you're getting out of there...even in dragon form."

Hope lit in his friend's eyes. "You done drinking?"

"For now."

"Then let's go," he said, rolling to his feet. "I want to inspect the fallout shelter. Assess what we'll need, and see my warriors."

"About that."

"What?"

"I've chosen the first three males."

"Let me guess—Azrad, Terranon and Kilmar."

He nodded. "Azrad's earned first pick."

"Good." Ivar held out his hand. Hamersveld grabbed hold. His friend yanked him to his feet. "And the other two?"

Hamersveld gestured to the door. "I'll fill you in on the way."

"Good enough."

Not even close.

With Natalie gone, nothing seemed as though it would ever be *good enough* again. At least, not for him. But as he followed Ivar out onto the deck, holding a picture of his female in his mind, satisfaction speared through him. She was safe. He'd done that—given her a fighting chance far from the harsh reality of Dragonkind.

With a murmur, he shucked his jeans and,

standing naked in the moonlight preparing to shift, decided *good enough* was all relative. Knowing she was driving toward a new life—one where she would be happy and free—gave him hope, lifted his spirits even as his heart ached and his dragon half mourned, knowing he'd never be whole without her.

12

MONTEREY, CALIFORNIA – SEVEN WEEKS LATER

Sitting in a posh armchair, Natalie stared at the degrees and diplomas hanging on the wall opposite her. Custom job, crisp white paper with stylized script protected by black wooden frames and sparkling glass, holding court in a place of prominence above an antique credenza. Inspired by Japanese art, if she had to guess, hand-carved dragons snarled from the front of wooden drawers. Her gaze swept the desk in front of her. Matching set. Another pretty piece with turned legs and polished wood, looking as fancy as the office she sat inside.

Not her first choice.

Given a half a chance, she would've been on the road by now, but...

She needed confirmation, a professional to tell her what her body already knew. To give reality a voice, say the truth out loud, in a way that couldn't be ignored, or denied.

A death grip on the slouchy handbag in her lap, Natalie shifted in her seat. She resisted reaching for her cellphone. Playing a game wouldn't ease her mind, and social media? Hell, online forums never helped. And besides, she wanted to be present. One hundred percent *here* when she heard the words that would change the course of her life...again...and—

The door opened behind her.

Straightening her spine, she looked over her shoulder.

Carrying a file, a woman entered the office. Curly hair pulled into a high ponytail, angular cheekbones leading the way, brown skin glowing with vitality, Dr. Angles crossed the room. As she rounded her desk, she met Natalie's gaze. Sage wisdom lay in those dark depths, unlocking worry, settling frayed nerves, helping reassure her. She picked the right place—the right person, a woman who would give it to her straight. No punches pulled, no information held in reserve.

Pushing stylish glasses up her nose, Dr. Angles sat behind the desk. She flipped through the file folder. Papers flapped as she pulled a couple of sheets from inside. "Well, you're healthy. Your blood work is normal. No underlying problems, but—"

"I'm pregnant," she said, gripping her bag tighter. Leather creaked. Natalie took a deep breath, waiting to be told, desperate for the words. Ever present over the last couple of weeks, nausea rolled in the pit of her stomach. "Right?"

Dr. Angles nodded. "Yes. You're pregnant."

Natalie closed her eyes. *Thank God. Thank God.* "Thank God."

A miracle. One Hamersveld assured her wasn't possible. Why he'd been so convinced he couldn't get her pregnant, Natalie didn't know, but...he was wrong. So very, very *wrong.*

Thank God.

Thank God.

Thank God.

"Happy," the doctor murmured. "Good to see. I wasn't sure how you'd take the news."

Taking a breath, Natalie opened her eyes. Of course, she was happy. Though, *thrilled* might be a better word to describe her state of being. How could she be anything else?

She thought about Hamersveld every day. Dreamed of him every night. Missed him so much, the pang grew more desperate by the hour, disrupting her so often it was a wonder she got anything done. The fact she managed to rent a small house—on the ocean like he requested—counted as a minor miracle. And forget about her part-time job fixing boat engines at the local marina. She'd fallen into that bit of luck without doing a thing, and still...she couldn't settle into her new life. Not completely. Never comfortably. Her yearning for him was too strong, making her look for reasons to ignore his warning and return to him.

And now, she had one—a baby.

His child. A tiny, future water dragon growing inside her. One she loved already.

Joy sparked through her. Natalie breathed through the emotion, so delighted she wanted to cry. "It's a surprise, Dr. Angles, but I'm happy."

"So I see, and not that it's any of my business, but... the father. Will he be involved?"

Her mouth curved. "Absolutely."

"Not a causal relationship, then."

"Nothing casual about him."

"Well, then," Dr. Angles said, sounding pleased for her. "Congratulations. I look forward to meeting him."

Natalie smiled. No chance of that happening.

Hamersveld didn't know where she'd landed, and as Dr. Angles got down to business, talking about prenatal vitamins, scheduling an ultrasound and future appointments, she almost regretted Hamersveld would never sit in a doctor's office with her. He would no doubt enjoy scaring the hell out of a human physician. He'd raise the poor woman's blood pressure, asking questions, demanding answers, scowling when he heard something he didn't like, his concern for her and his child leading the way.

Imagining it, Natalie almost laughed.

She swallowed her amusement at the last second and tuned back in, listening to Dr. Angles lecture her about safety—what to eat, activities to avoid, and getting enough sleep. Natalie catalogued it all, filing the information away to draw from later, knowing she would need it. The moment she broke through the five-hundred-mile marker, and Hamersveld sensed her, she'd need to batten down the hatches.

His reaction would be legendary. One for the record books. His desire to protect her so strong, he'd overreact. Snarl and growl, stomp and shout, while lecturing her. Which meant she must be prepared. For anything. Whatever argument he threw at her.

Possessing answers to all his questions—along with buckets full of patience—was paramount. The key to calming his fears and getting him to listen while she explained her reason for returning to Seattle, but...

God.

Pressing her hands to her belly, Natalie grinned. She couldn't wait to see his face when she told him he'd been wrong—that miracles really did happen, and she carried his child.

ALSO BY COREENE CALLAHAN

Dragonfury Scotland
Fury of a Highland Dragon
Fury of Shadows
Fury of Denial
Fury of Persuasion

"Villains" of the Dragonfury Series
Fury of Fate
Fury of Conviction

Dragonfury Series
Fury of Fire
Fury of Ice
Fury of Seduction
Fury of Desire
Fury of Obsession
Fury of Surrender
Fury of Destruction

Circle of Seven Series
Knight Awakened
Knight Avenged

Warriors of the Realm Series
Warrior's Revenge

ABOUT THE AUTHOR

Coreene Callahan is the bestselling author of the Dragonfury Novels and Circle of Seven Series, in which she combines her love of romance and adventure with her passion for history. After graduating with honors in psychology and taking a detour to work in interior design, Coreene finally returned to her first love: writing. Her debut novel, *Fury of Fire* was a finalist in the New Jersey Romance Writers Golden Leaf Contest in two categories: Best First Book and Best Paranormal. She lives in Canada with her family, a spirited Anatolian Shepard, and her wild imaginary world.